ROSANNE BITTNER

WHERE
Heaven
BEGINS

Steeple
Hill®

Published by Steeple Hill Books™

To my special and beautiful grandsons, Brennan, Connor and
Blake Bittner; and to their parents, son Brock and wife, Lori,
and son Brian and wife, Edna. When I'm down, all I need
is to hear the words "Gwamma, I wuv you," and I'm
on top of the world again. I'm sure that in the future one
of my inspirational stories will involve the love between a
grandmother and her grandson. My own grandsons are
the light of my life and truly a gift from God.

STEEPLE HILL BOOKS

Steeple
Hill®

ISBN-13: 978-0-373-78595-7
ISBN-10:   0-373-78595-X

WHERE HEAVEN BEGINS

Copyright © 2004 by Rosanne Bittner

Printed in U.S.A.

AUTHOR'S NOTE

Within most of my fifty-plus novels about America's history there has always been an element of faith that was important to each story. When the opportunity arose for me to write for Steeple Hill, I was delighted, as deep inside I have always wanted my writing to inspire hope and faith within the reader. I am deeply gratified to have often accomplished that, or so many of my readers have told me.

Now, by writing for a line designed especially for books with faith in God as the primary theme, I am free to release that little voice inside that has been telling me that this is the kind of book I must write.

In these times when it is important to remember that through all the upheaval in the world today, we can still realize peace and joy deep inside through abiding faith, it is my privilege to write a story that is centered on faith in God.

All Scripture verses used in this novel are taken from the King James version of the Holy Bible.

A good share of the travel details in this novel were gleaned from the authentic diaries of E. Hazard Wells, a reporter who traveled to the Klondike in 1897 and whose notes were published in *Magnificence and Misery*, edited by Randall M. Dodd, Doubleday & Co., Inc., 1984.

As a reader for whom faith in God is a key element in daily life, you will, I hope, find *Where Heaven Begins* worthwhile reading and an uplifting experience.

Rosanne Bittner

ACKNOWLEDGMENTS

To all those who have touched my life in a positive way without even knowing it. I can only hope to do the same in return through my writing.

A special thank-you also to Ann Leslie Tuttle, the editor who originally brought Rosanne Bittner to Steeple Hill; and to my agent, Denise Marcil, for suggesting I try writing an inspirational book. Writing this novel has opened up a whole new avenue in writing for me. I have loved every minute of it.

And who can write an inspirational novel without thanking God for a talent that comes only from Him. I thank Him too for planting the seed of faith that helped me write this book.

Chapter One

Be not a witness against thy neighbor without cause;
And deceive not with thy lips.
                                    —Proverbs 24:28

San Francisco, August 4, 1898

"We've taken a vote, Elizabeth. We understand you will need to find a job and a place to live, and we are ready to help you there, but you will have to leave Reverend Selby's residence."

Elizabeth Breckenridge felt as though the blood was leaving her body, beginning with her head and draining down toward her feet. She had no doubt what had caused this meeting of church deacons who sat circled around her with looks of condemnation on their faces.

"May I have an explanation?" she asked, fighting not to cry. Elizabeth always cried when she was extremely angry, but she refused to shed tears in front of these pious judges, especially the two-faced Reverend Selby. *Lord, help me not to hate these men.*

"Surely you know the reason for this." The words came from Anderson Williams, who'd once been a good friend to her father.

Liz faced him squarely. "And surely you know me better," she answered. "How can you do this, Mr. Williams? You were one of my father's staunchest supporters. You know my family well, and you know how I was brought up."

Williams shifted uncomfortably, and Liz could see that he was bound to abide by the decision of the rest of these church leaders, six deacons in all. And, of course, the Reverend Thomas Selby himself sat in judgment.

"I'm sorry, Elizabeth, but I do understand it's possible after all that's happened to you that…well, my dear…it would only be natural for you to turn to someone for comfort, and perhaps for you to…well…yearn for the safety and steadfastness of a man's love," Williams said.

"Love? Is that what Reverend Selby told you? That I turned to him for comfort? That I said I *loved* him?" Still fighting tears, Elizabeth continued. "Gentlemen, my father always taught that we should not condemn. According to St. John, Chapter 7, Verse 24, *Judge not the appearance, but judge righteous judgment. You* have made a grave *misjudgment*, I can assure you. I am not the one who should be cast out of this church, but I can already see that none of you is ready to listen to the truth, so I will not sit here and beg you to believe me! Only our Holy Father knows the truth, and true judgment will prevail when all of you stand before Him!" She turned her gaze to Reverend Selby.

"Including *you*, Reverend, but I forgive you, *for if ye forgive not men their trespasses, neither will your Father forgive your trespasses*. St. Matthew, Chapter 6, Verse 15."

Reverend Selby's dark eyes narrowed with what Liz interpreted as a literal threat. "We all understand your sad situation, child."

"My sad situation?" Oh, how hard it was to hold her tongue! That had always been difficult, and right now the Lord was not helping her at all when it came to not harboring hatred and a desire for revenge against the reverend. Deep in her heart she really could *not* forgive this man! "For one thing, I am not a child. I am twenty years old."

She turned her attention to the others, men who had known her since she was a little girl; men who had worked with her father to build this church in San Francisco; men who now fell into the common belief that all women were basically weak and needy and were somehow responsible for any man's basic weaknesses. "My sad situation is not the awfulness of losing both my parents to death and my brother to a higher calling," she continued. "My saddest situation is that I accepted the reverend's offer to remain living with him and his wife until I could get back on my feet and decide what to do next after Mother's death. My saddest situation results from trusting a supposedly godly man and thinking he truly wanted to help me. I misjudged his kindness. Reverend Selby had in mind when he offered his home to me other intentions than just helping the daughter of your former preacher!"

"Daughter, watch your tongue!" The words came from Cletus Olson, another former friend of her father's. "Don't add false accusations to what has already happened. We are ready to forgive and help you."

Liz rose from the straight-backed oak chair in which she sat. She felt like an accused harlot. She took a deep breath, astounded and disappointed at the attitude of these men who'd known her family so well.

"Speaking of false accusations, I can only imagine what the pious reverend has been telling you," she said, turning to meet the eyes of each man directly. "I need no forgiveness, and it sickens me that you would believe him. I assure you that I will gladly leave his home, and in fact I was about to tell all of you the same…that it might be best if I lived elsewhere."

She swallowed, realizing now that this was God's way of letting her know it was time to act on what she'd been wanting to do for a long time. "I had already decided to join my brother in Dawson. I know that many of you believe he only went there to search for gold like all the thousands of others who've gone, but I know in my heart he intended to build a church and minister to the many lost souls who will surely need his services. I've heard some of you joking about his real intentions, but you know what a sincere man of God he is, how hard he worked to save this church after Father was killed. He would never drop all of that for something as shallow as a gold rush. He felt God's calling and he followed it. I intend to go and find him."

"How on earth will you get there, Elizabeth?" Anderson Williams frowned with what seemed true concern. "It's a terribly dangerous trip for a young woman alone. Besides, it's too late in the year to go at all."

Liz held her chin proudly. "That shouldn't concern any of you, considering that you are so eager to ban me from the reverend's house and brand me as something I am not. Traveling to the Yukon won't be any worse than struggling to find work and fend for myself with absolutely no family left here…and a congregation that is apparently whispering behind my back."

Elizabeth folded her arms, angry with herself for not speaking up sooner about Reverend Selby instead of keeping quiet and allowing him the chance to speak first and turn everyone against her. It had always been obvious to her that the man was jealous of the fact that her father had founded Christ Church, and that her presence reminded the congregation of that. Selby didn't just want to preach here. He wanted to "own" Christ Church and its members. He didn't want to be known as the man who tried to fill Reverend William Breckenridge's shoes. He wanted all the glory for himself. He'd done what he could to malign the Breckenridge name and get rid of the last bit of Breckenridge influence in this church so that he and no other would be the number-one leader of his flock. Winning over these men, former friends of her father's, was his final victory.

"We've taken a collection for you, Elizabeth," Jeffrey Clay spoke up. He was always the most quiet, reasonable man among the deacons. "It was intended to help you find a boarding house and keep you on your feet until you could find a way to support yourself, perhaps by teaching. If you choose to use the money to get you to Alaska, that's your choice." He rose and cleared his throat, walking up to her and handing over an envelope. "There is four hundred dollars here. That should be of considerable help. We are aware that your mother also saved some money, which she put in your name before she died."

Elizabeth took the money with a gloved hand. "I am told that traveling to Alaska could take much more than this, what with the embellished prices of goods there. But somehow I'll make it with this and what little else I have. I apparently have no choice."

She turned to leave, wanting nothing more now than to get away from the accusing glares of these pompous men who knew nothing of what she'd suffered since her mother had died three months ago. She should be angry with her brother. This was partly his fault. If he hadn't up and left last summer... Oh, Peter, if only you were here, none of this would have happened!

"Elizabeth, wait!"

Liz stopped short at the sound of Reverend Selby's booming voice. Even before he'd started making advances toward her, he'd always had a way of looking at her as though she were some kind of evil temptress. She turned to glare back at him.

"Our love and prayers go with you, daughter," the reverend told her. "Know that I forgive you, as does my wife. You are welcome to stay another few days until you can make your arrangements, or until you find work. Surely you could teach, or perhaps work as a nanny. And there are any number of young men in our fold who would like to court you. Marriage could bring you all the security you desire."

Oh, Lord, why are You making it so impossible not to hate this liar!

"I'll not marry just for security," she answered aloud. "And yes, I will look for work, but not in San Francisco. I'll not stay here any longer than it will take me to go home and pack my things. I'll find a hotel room for tonight and however many days it takes to procure passage to Seattle. I'll leave as soon as I can!" She moved her gaze about the circle of men again. "And how dare any of you talk about forgiving me! *I* am not the one who needs forgiving! I am the one who will be praying that God forgives all of *you* for what you've done today!"

With that, Elizabeth quickly left the brick building that had been built next to Christ Church as a gathering hall for potlucks and the like. She rushed around behind it, clinging to the envelope of money. She let the tears come then, deep sobs of humiliation, disappointment, mourning for her dead father and mother, and fear of the unknown. What choice did she have now but to go and find Peter? All she wanted was to be with her brother, the only family she had left.

"Lord Jesus, help me do this," she wept. How afraid Jesus Himself must have been so many times, but He trusted God to give Him the strength and wisdom necessary to bear the accusations thrown at Him, and to travel where others dared not go. Now Elizabeth knew that she must do the same.

Chapter Two

*Thou hast rebuked the proud that are cursed,
which do err from Thy commandments. Remove
from me reproach and contempt; for I have kept
Thy testimonies.*

—Psalms 119:21 & 22

Feeling guilty over her anger, too guilty even to pray about it, Elizabeth stuffed clothing into two worn carpet bags that had belonged to her mother. Tears stung her eyes at the longing in her heart to be able to turn to the woman now. The day three years ago that the police informed the family that Liz's father had been murdered was the day Edna Breckenridge's health began slipping downhill. She never really recovered from the loss of her husband, but she insisted that no one in the family lose faith in God because of it.

Still, this last hurt did indeed bring a challenge to Elizabeth's own faith. What more terrible things lay in wait for her? What had she done to deserve this? First, her father, a faithful servant of the Lord, cruelly murdered while bravely ministering to miserable drunks and thieves and prostitutes who plied their dastardly trades on the Barbary Coast. Then her brother, another faithful servant of the Lord, as well as her best friend, felt a calling to follow the hordes of men headed for the Yukon to find gold. God meant for Peter to go there, too, and to build a church and bring His word to men who would too easily forget God even existed in their quest to get rich, or so her brother believed.

After Peter left, one of the more respected deacons, Thomas Selby, had offered to take over as preacher for the church. Deep inside, Liz had always suspected Selby of wanting the job even when her father was alive. Even her mother had doubted that Selby had anything like the abiding faith and love for mankind in his heart that Liz's father had possessed.

"They'll never replace Reverend William Breckenridge," Elizabeth seethed. She closed one carpet bag and threw her only other pair of shoes into the second bag. Her whole family had given up so much so that the church could grow, to the point that they had few possessions. She and her mother had been allowed to continue living upstairs in the parsonage after Thomas Selby became the new minister, but her mother's health failed rapidly and the woman eventually died from what the doctor claimed was cancer. It was a long, painful, cruel death, another blow to Elizabeth's faith.

Now this. So unfair! Thinking she was some kind of helpless, needy waif, the pious Reverend Selby had "consoled" Elizabeth with a little too much hugging and touching, as far as she was concerned. It was not until the night one week ago when the man had come into her bedroom and sat on the edge of her bed, waking her when he leaned close and tried talking her into letting him "help" her by coming to bed and "filling her with his strength" that Liz had realized the man's true intentions.

She'd screamed for him to get out, pushed at him, her reaction waking the man's wife. The false accusations that came out of the reverend's mouth then had shocked her. Of course, his wife believed him when he'd told her that Elizabeth had asked him to come to her room to pray with her and then had tried to tempt him into her bed.

She shuddered at the mere thought of the much older, supposedly righteous man being such a hypocrite. He had two grown sons older than she was, and he'd even preached sermons about the sin of adultery! After the incident, Mrs. Selby and other women in the congregation, women who'd been friends of her mother's and who'd often offered their help in her grief, became cold towards her.

Oh, how it hurt to lose not only her beloved father and mother, but to be lied about and thus to lose others who had been her only source of comfort. Before the disgusting meeting with the deacons today Elizabeth had already decided to leave San Francisco and go to live with Peter. She'd received letters from him, knew he had indeed founded a church in Dawson. He most surely would not want her to make the trip, but he had no choice in the matter. Once she made up her mind to do something, she did it! Her mother used to tease her about such stubbornness.

She drew in her breath and closed her eyes. *"God,*

forgive me," she prayed. *"I have never been so full of anger and...hatred. Yes, that's what it is, Lord. It's hatred. I'm so sorry that I feel this way."* She went to her knees. *"Please guide me in my journey, Lord. Help me make it safely to Alaska. Help me find my brother. Show me what it is You want of me. Take away this anger so that I can better serve You with a heart that is not full of malice."*

She moved to sit down on the bed, reaching to take her Bible from the nightstand. She pressed it to her heart and let the tears come. Oh, how she missed the days when her family was all together, working hard to build their own church. Since she was eight years old, when her family had arrived in San Francisco after an arduous journey by wagon from Illinois, a life of serving the Lord was all she'd known. She'd been so involved with helping first her father and then her brother that she'd never even taken time for her own life, for allowing young men to court her or attending any social functions except those involving the church. She'd taught Sunday school, helped her mother minister to sick members and then had spent months nursing her own mother until she died.

"Why, God? Haven't I served You well? Why have You taken so much from me?"

She opened her Bible to the New Testament, always believing that wherever she opened the Gospels she would find answers to her problems. She believed it was God's way of talking to her, leading her.

"Beware, lest any man spoil you through philosophy and vain deceit," she read, "after the tradition of men, after the rudiments of the world, and not after Christ."

There, as always, was her answer. She could not allow the hypocrites who'd kicked her out of this parsonage to spoil her faith.

She closed her eyes. *"Lord, I believe You have a reason for the turns life hands us. Surely You mean for me to go to Dawson. I'm afraid, Lord, but I know You will be with me. And I believe there is a purpose for what has happened that You have not yet shown me. Whatever You have planned, Lord, I will accept whatever You entrust to me."*

She rose and packed the Bible into the second carpet bag, along with what was left of her clothing, such as it was. Her family had never owned many material things, and she dressed simply. She breathed deeply as she buckled the second bag, feeling more confident now. God had a purpose for her. She did not doubt it.

She walked to the dresser where she used to sit while her mother brushed her hair for her, always praising its thickness and luster—*a lovely red glint to your dark tresses when the sun hits your hair just right*, her mother would say. Liz sometimes felt guilty for admiring her own hair during those times, but she was proud of it, and it felt good to remember how she and her mother used to talk about so many things, and to remember how kind and loving Edna Breckenridge had been.

A lump rose in her throat at the memory. She tied on her bonnet, remembering her mother's warning to always wear a hat with a brim to *protect the beautiful, flawless skin God gave you. When the Lord blesses you with good health, you should respect your body and take care of it.* That included, of course, giving her body to a man someday only out of love and through God's divine blessing. So far she'd not met one young man who came close to giving her even the slightest feelings of desire in that respect. And the night Reverend Selby had come into her room with his hideous suggestions only made the thought of being with any man repulsive. It would be a long time before she forgot that awful night!

She forced back another urge to cry as she smoothed her plain green dress with a tiny white ruffle at the high neck. It matched her small green pill bonnet. She wore black ankle-high button shoes and looked properly prim and respectable, certainly not the harlot the Reverend Selby had tried to convince others she was.

It was midafternoon. Neither the Reverend nor Mrs. Selby were home. Good. She'd not bother telling them or anyone else goodbye. She'd go to the church graveyard and visit her father's and mother's graves one more time. Oh, how it would make her heart ache to leave them and Christ Church behind, but she had no choice now. They would want her to be with Peter. Steamships left every day for Alaska; and she'd pay passage on one of them and leave.

She took a last look at the room she'd occupied since she was a little girl and shared with her mother for those last months of suffering. Then she straightened, hooking the strings of her handbag on her arm, a handbag that carried all the money she possessed in the world. She picked up her carpet bags and turned, walking out the door. This was it. There was no turning back.

Chapter Three

I am a stranger in the earth; hide not Thy
commandments from me.
—Psalms 119:19

August or not, it was foggy and chilly today. Elizabeth was not unaware of the stares of the hundreds of men who milled about. She could not forget the letter she'd received just this past spring from Peter, in which he'd casually stated that any women who came unescorted to Alaska were generally considered to be there for prostitution, although a very few managed to open legitimate businesses such as eateries, or to find work as seamstresses.

Elizabeth had practically memorized Peter's letters, of which she had only two. It was not easy getting mail out of Dawson and all the way down to San Francisco. She'd received one letter over the winter after his arrival last fall, and the more recent one this spring. She'd written Peter right away about their mother's death, and it was possible he'd not even received that letter yet, let alone the letter she'd written two nights ago.

Now she stood on the wharf waiting for passengers to disembark the *Alaskan Damsel,* a steamer that had made numerous trips to Seattle and on to Skagway via the Inside Passage throughout the past two summers.

As she'd suspected would be the case, not many people left the boat, yet hundreds waited, ready to board. For most who made this journey, it was a one-way trip, and like most of them, she'd purchased a one-way ticket herself. Once she found Peter, she had no intention of ever returning to San Francisco.

She shivered from the damp fog, then jumped when the high smokestacks of the *Damsel* billowed black smoke, accompanied by three shrill whistles, beckoning all who intended to board her. She wondered if that included the three painted, gaudily dressed women who stood not far away batting their eyes at some of the men. It made her ill to think what such women did to make their money. Not far from them stood a group of Chinese, conversing in their strange sing-song tongue. The men's hair was worn long and braided into tails at the backs of their necks. Other Chinese as well as black men worked at the docks loading and unloading supplies.

Different. All so different. Did God actually expect his followers to love people like that? She liked to think that she could, but if she actually had to associate with them… *Oh, Lord, I fall so short of Your will. I am surrounded by heathens and harlots and men whose hearts are filled with a lust for gold and painted women. How can I truly love*

such people? I know that I am no better than they, and yet
it is so hard to think of them as equals. Teach me how to
love all people.

Perhaps if her father had not been murdered by people
very much like these…. The memory still brought a
stabbing pain to her heart. Her father used to come home
and ask the family to pray for thieves and murderers, al-
coholics and drug users, harlots and men who visited them.
He'd truly been a man of God, for she believed he honestly
loved these people in the way God intended. He'd died
serving the Lord. The same people to whom he'd mini-
stered had turned around and murdered him for a mere
three dollars. They had even stolen his clothing, leaving
him naked and disgraced.

To realize God meant her to love that kind of people
brought a great struggle to her soul. The congregation
mourned, but they also had repeatedly warned her father
not to go to such dangerous places as the Barbary Coast, a
section of this dock area not so far away from here. No one
else in her father's church, most certainly not Reverend
Selby and the deacons, had anywhere near the courage of
her father when it came to bringing God's Word to the lost
souls of the world. The remaining members of Christ
Church had decided it was best simply to serve the current
congregation and the surrounding, more civilized neighbor-
hood. If anyone on the Barbary Coast wanted to find God,
they were welcome to come to the church and be saved.

Only her brother understood what their father's calling
was all about. He was following William Breckenridge's
footsteps, heading into dangerous, wild country just to

minister to those who would have no other source of hearing God's Word.

She took a deep breath, praying she could drum up the same courage it would take to make this journey. Baggage and supplies were being unloaded from the boat, as well as several large, well-guarded crates that took several men to load onto wagons.

Gold ore? She'd heard that thousands, maybe even millions of dollars worth of the treasured ore arrived almost daily in Seattle and San Francisco, to be shipped to stamp mills. Her brother's last letter revealed that stamp mills were already being built in the Yukon so that the ore could be processed there. Rumors of the value of the gold coming out of the mines in the Yukon abounded. It was difficult to know what to believe.

The crowd around her grew more excited as they watched the armed bank guards that surrounded the ore wagons. Men began shouting about gold and getting rich, whooping and laughing.

"I ain't never gonna have to work again!" one man yelled.

"I'll build my Sarah the biggest house in San Francisco!" yelled another.

Elizabeth began to see what the term *gold fever* meant. Why was being rich so important? She thought about how Christ had never owned a thing to His name but the clothes He wore and the sandals on His feet. If her brother were to, by chance, find gold, he would use it to build his church and help the poor.

The wharf gradually became even more crowded. The wagons surrounded by men with rifles rumbled past, and

Elizabeth picked up both her carpet bags and made her way
to a less-congested area, getting bumped and shoved as she
struggled through the crowd, keeping the *Alaskan Damsel*
in sight so she could get on board as soon as the boat took
on its passengers. She'd paid the cheapest rate possible,
deciding she would have to bear the discomfort of sleeping
below deck using one of her bags as a pillow. She would
need the greater share of her money once she arrived in
Skagway for the clothing and supplies it would take to
make the journey to the Klondike, or so she'd been told by
the man who'd sold her the steamer ticket. He'd advised
her not to make the trip at all, most certainly not alone, but
she'd made up her mind and there was no going back. She
might end up stranded in Skagway without enough money
to go any farther, but at least there she'd be closer to Peter.

"God will guide me," she'd told the man. Deep inside
she struggled against fear and doubt, secretly praying
almost constantly for the Lord to help her do this.

She removed one glove and ran her fingers over the
buttons of the bodice of her dress, making sure none had
come undone. Today she wore a simple gray frock with a
black velvet shawl and black velvet hat, wanting to appear
as plain as possible to make sure strange men realized she
was a proper lady. Her hair was wound into a bun at the
base of her neck, and she checked to be sure the pins were
still holding it tight. It was so thick she always had diffi-
culty holding it in place, whether with pins or combs.

Her handbag dangling from her arm, she reached behind
her neck to tighten the hairpins when suddenly her arm was
jerked painfully backward and her handbag ripped away.

She screamed with the pain, then took no time to stop and think. Her money! It was all in that handbag! Following her first basic instinct, she ran after the culprit who'd stolen all the money she had in the world, screaming for him to stop, screaming to others please to stop him for her.

Dear Lord, please stop him! Please don't let this happen! Help me!

She began screaming the words aloud. "Help! Help! Please stop him!"

It was then that someone rushed past her and tackled the thief, throwing him to the wooden planks of the pier, then jerking him up and landing several vicious blows, bloodying the man's nose and mouth. Her apparent aide was tall and obviously strong and knew what he was about, for his blows were well aimed and the thief had no chance against him. Then, to Elizabeth's wide-eyed shock, the stranger picked up the thief and threw him over the edge of the dock into the water.

He whirled then, as two more ragged-looking men approached him with knives. The stranger whipped out the six-gun he wore at his hip so quickly that Elizabeth barely saw the movement.

"Back off!" he ordered.

The two men looked at each other and backed away. Still holding the gun on them, the stranger walked over to pick up Elizabeth's handbag and a wide-brimmed hat that had been knocked from his own head in the fight. His two would-be attackers melted into the crowd that had gathered to watch, and finally the stranger holstered his sidearm. He put his hat on and stepped up to Elizabeth, still breathing hard, a slight bruise forming on his square jaw. He held out the handbag. "I believe this belongs to you, ma'am."

Speechless, Elizabeth took the bag, staring into deep-blue eyes that looked back at her from beneath the hat that now covered wild, wavy strands of dark hair. He was the best-looking man Elizabeth had ever seen, and she felt a sudden, inexplicable jolt to her heart.

Chapter Four

❧

If thine enemy be hungry, give him bread to eat;
and if he be thirsty, give him water to drink...
—Proverbs 25:21

The savior of Elizabeth's handbag began to walk away before she found her voice. "Mister, wait!"

From several feet ahead the man turned, pushing back his hat slightly and looking her over. Elizabeth wondered if perhaps he thought her one of the loose women heading for the gold fields. Surely not! Who could think such a thing, the way she was dressed? No matter what he thought, she had to at least thank him, but... "What about that man you threw into the water? He could drown!" she called to him.

The stranger frowned. "Who cares? Any man who steals from a woman is worthless anyway. You of all people shouldn't be concerned with what happens to him."

"But...he's a human being. If he drowns, I'll be responsible!"

"What?" He grunted a laugh. "He stole your purse, and *I'm* the one who threw him into the water."

Elizabeth glanced toward the spot where the man had been thrown off. She noticed a couple of men helping him climb back onto the wharf.

"There, you see? He's wet and mad, but he's all right. The water probably helped sober him up," the stranger told her.

The voice was closer, and Elizabeth turned to see him standing right before her. It was then she realized he was a good six feet tall and well built. She backed away slightly. "Well, I...I'm glad, in spite of what he did. And I thank you, sir, for recovering my handbag. All the money I have in the world is in it."

He grinned and shook his head. "Then I suggest you take that money and put it inside your girdle or your camisole, someplace where a man can't get to it so easily." He frowned teasingly then. "Unless, of course, you're not the prim-and-proper lady you appear to be."

Elizabeth reddened. "I beg your pardon!"

He tipped his hat. "Just some friendly advice, ma'am." He started away again.

"What's your name?" Elizabeth called after him.

Again he turned, removing his hat and running a hand through his thick hair. "Clint Brady."

Still feeling heat in her cheeks, Elizabeth nodded to him. "Well, thank you again, Mr. Brady. I'll...take your advice."

Brady looked around and stepped closer again. "You headed for Alaska?"

Elizabeth nodded. "Yes. My brother is building a church in the Yukon. I am going to join him."

The man frowned, his blue eyes revealing true concern. *"Alone?"*

Elizabeth glanced down at his gun and suddenly wondered if she was revealing too much information. Still, he'd risked his life to get her purse back for her. "Yes."

"And your brother approves?"

"He doèsn't know. I sent him a letter, but I'll be well on my way by the time he gets it. He'll have no choice in the matter. He's all the family I have left and I'm going. God will get me there safely."

Brady's eyebrows arched quizzically, and Elizabeth could see he thought she was silly to make such a remark. "He will, will He?" He chuckled. "Well, ma'am…what's your name, anyway?"

"Elizabeth Breckenridge."

"Well, Miss Breckenridge, it's nice to have so much faith, but if I were you, I'd still be more careful of my money. And I'd find a guide of some kind. The trip to the Yukon is daunting for the strongest of men, let alone a woman on her own. You able to carry a thousand pounds of supplies on your back up a mountainside?"

Elizabeth swallowed. "Well, I…I'll find a way. Perhaps I'll find a guide once I reach Skagway…and a mule or a horse."

"Mmm-hmm. And how are you going to know who to trust?"

She held her chin higher with pretended confidence. "I'll know, that's all. However, I doubt I have enough money to pay a man for such work anyway. Perhaps someone will take me for the cost of his own supplies… grubstaking, I think they call it."

Brady nodded. "That's what they call it." He looked around the crowd as though watching for someone in particular. "Come on. I'll walk you back to your bags, if they're still there."

"Oh, my goodness! I forgot all about them! What if someone has stolen them!" Elizabeth began a rushed walk back to where she'd left her things, and Clint Brady walked beside her.

"They're probably all right," he tried to assure her. "Believe it or not, most of the men headed for the Yukon are just common good men, a lot of them family men who respect proper ladies." Elizabeth's bags came into sight. "There, you see?"

"Thank you, Jesus," Elizabeth said as she hurried up to the bags and picked them up. People were now boarding the *Damsel.* "I'd better get on board." She looked up at Clint Brady. "Thank you again, Mr. Brady. I didn't even ask if you're all right."

"Oh, I've been through worse, believe me."

"Oh, my." She glanced at his gun again. She wanted to ask more, but it might seem too intrusive; besides, there was no time. She had to get on board. She smiled nervously and nodded a goodbye, turning and climbing the wooden plank that led to the steamer's wooden deck. The *Damsel* was one of the larger steamers available, painted bright yellow with white trim, three stories of expensive cabins looking inviting. Again, Elizabeth wished she could afford a cabin, rather than staying below deck.

Only God knew how she was going to reach her destination safely—or if she would reach it at all. She had to

keep the faith. Whatever was God's will for her, so be it.
Fate, or more likely God, had led her this far.

She stood at the rail of the ship for several more long
minutes, staring out at the hilly streets of San Francisco.
So many memories there, mostly good ones until her father
had been murdered. And Mama. Her eyes stung with tears.
Mama! She might never again be able to visit her mother's
grave. Oh, how she missed her! She could not imagine
finding happiness here ever again. Her only hope for that
was to be with Peter.

Her heart rushed faster when the steamer again blasted
three short whistles from its tall smokestacks. Several black
men working along the wharf unwrapped heavy rope from
around thick wooden dock posts and tossed them to the
deck of the *Damsel*. Elizabeth noticed again what a montage
of races mingled at the wharf, and that many of them had
boarded the *Damsel*. Negroes, Chinese, painted women, a
couple of men who looked Indian, perhaps even Eskimos.
She realized that in all the years she'd lived here, she really
couldn't tell one Indian tribe from another. She only knew
that most of the California tribes had become nearly extinct
from war and disease. And, of course, there were many
Spaniards among the crowd and several on board.

She realized that the members of Christ Church were
nearly all white, and that many of them did not openly
welcome other races. Her father would have welcomed
anyone, and he'd died going out to find those who truly
needed to hear God's Word. Since his death the church had
strayed far from what her father meant it to be. He would
expect his children to love and welcome other races, for he'd

often preached that Christ taught that all should love one another, no matter how different that other person might be.

She turned to glance around at those who'd boarded the *Damsel*, and there were those very three women! And standing there talking to them was none other than Clint Brady! She'd not even noticed him come aboard.

So, he, too, was going to Alaska. To look for gold? She suspected it was for some other reason. Why did he wear a gun at his side? She couldn't remember seeing a badge on the man, but maybe he was a lawman. That would explain why he knew how to handle her attacker. He obviously had a good side to him, or he wouldn't have helped her…but he also had a violent side…and apparently a sinful side, or he wouldn't be standing there talking to harlots!

Why did that bother her? It was ridiculous to care. He glanced her way, and again she felt that little jolt to her heart, that little, uneasy feeling that Clint Brady had some kind of connection to her…some strange reason for coming into her life in such an odd way.

She turned away. How silly! Besides, the man might only be going as far as Seattle. Still, why did she actually feel relieved that he was on board?

Slowly the docks of San Francisco Bay began to disappear into the cold mist. The sound of other steamers' shrill whistles pierced the thick fog that began to shroud the *Damsel*.

She was on her way. *Stay with me, Jesus. I'm so afraid. My strength and courage come only from You.*

Chapter Five

*And the scribes and Pharisees brought unto him a
woman taken in adultery; and when they had set
her in the midst, they said unto him, Master, this
woman was taken in adultery, in the very act...such
should be stoned; but what sayest thou?
...Jesus...said unto them, He that is without sin
among you, let him first cast a stone at her.... And
they...went out one by one.... And Jesus said to the
woman, where are thine accusers? Hath no man
condemned thee? She said, No man, Lord. And
Jesus said unto her, Neither do I condemn thee:
go, and sin no more.*

—St. John 8:3-11

Elizabeth studied her Bible by lantern light, the only
kind of light available on the lower deck, although the
cabins and upper decks had electric lights, for what that
was worth. For the first two days of the trip men grum-

bled that the lights constantly dimmed or went out completely.

Elizabeth could barely sleep because of the deck's vibration, due to the steamer's engines rumbling directly beneath her. Added to that noise was the noise of others talking, particularly the painted women who were situated only a few feet from her. The first night they'd laughed and visited half the night, talking about things that made Elizabeth feel like a sinner just by hearing them.

Then last night the women had put up a makeshift tent made of blankets, and one of them lay inside the tent groaning in pain most of the night. The other two sat just outside the blankets whispering about something. Elizabeth assumed the woman groaning must be sick to her stomach from something she ate.

She fished through one of her carpet bags and took out a bottle of ink and a pen, as well as a notebook she'd purchased before leaving San Francisco. She had decided to keep a diary of her journey, partly to keep herself occupied so she wouldn't think about all the frightening things that could happen to her, and also because if she died on this journey, someone might send the diary on to Peter as a keepsake. She began by writing a note as to what to do with the journal should she not make it to Dawson.

August 10, 1898…This is only my third day, and we should make Seattle very soon. This part of my journey is, of course, the easy part, but I will try to make note of what happens every day. So far, other than when a thief tried to steal my handbag before I could board the steamer, things have been quite uneventful.

I am camping here below deck with Chinese and Indians and even three painted women whose occupation I suspect is unmentionable. One of them is sick. I have no idea…

She set her pen aside when she noticed that one of the painted women was coming toward her with what looked like a wadded-up towel.

"Miss?"

Elizabeth swallowed. Should she be seen associating with such women? Don't forget the adulteress, and how Jesus forgave her. She capped her pen and set it and her diary aside. "Yes?"

The woman crouched closer, and in the lantern light Elizabeth realized the woman was not much older than she was!

"My name is Collette. My friend in the tent over there that we set up, her name is Francine." Collette kept her voice lowered. She looked around, as though keeping a big secret. "My other friend there is Tricia, and we were all wondering…I mean…we've noticed you reading a Bible and all…and maybe you know enough about it to… well…pray over a dead body."

Elizabeth's eyes widened in surprise. "Did Francine *die?*"

"Oh, no, miss," Collette answered in a near whisper. "I think she'll be all right. We have experience in these things. That's not what we'd want you to pray about…except, of course, if you'd be so kind as to do that. Francine just lost a baby. I've got it right here in this towel. There's not much to it, but, well, you know, it just doesn't seem right not to pray over it, 'cause it's still what's left of a little human life. But me, I'm not much good at such things, so I thought maybe you'd consider coming up top with me and saying a prayer before I drop it into the water—kind of a burial at sea I guess you'd say."

Elizabeth felt her heart pounding in her chest. *Dear Lord, help me know what to do!* This woman of the streets was asking her to pray over an illegitimate child delivered by yet another prostitute! "I…well, I…"

"I know it seems awful to somebody like you, but like the Good Book says, we're all God's children, even this tiny little bit of life that's hardly recognizable. I sure don't intend just to throw it in the garbage."

Elizabeth wondered at the fact that the woman seemed to understand a little bit about God and the Bible, and she actually respected the bit of life she held in the towel. She felt ashamed about worrying what others would think of talking to such women. God surely was placing this duty in her hands, and so she would pray over the poor little soul in the towel. She reminded herself as she stood up that her father would have done the same. "I…of course I'll pray over the baby, and I'll pray for its mother. Are you sure she's all right…physically, I mean?"

"I think she'll be all right, but there's an awful lot of bleeding. We're getting off in Seattle to get her some help. It's kind of you to ask." Collette leaned a little closer. "And we understand somebody like you wouldn't want to be seen consorting with us, so I won't bother you after you do this one thing."

"It's all right. My father was a preacher, and he used to minister to people along the Barbary Coast."

Collette brightened, raising painted eyebrows. "Well, he must have been a real good man."

"Yes, he was." Elizabeth realized she needed to think about what God's love truly means. "Let's go to the main deck," she told Collette.

Nervous and unsure, Elizabeth led Collette to the main deck. It was early morning and the sea was quite calm today. They managed to find a place away from others, as many men were still asleep and not milling about. Elizabeth touched the towel and prayed for God to bless the bit of life inside and take him or her into His arms for blessed eternity.

"'Suffer the little children and forbid them not to come unto me,'" she said after praying, "'for of such is the Kingdom of Heaven.'" She noticed tears in Collette's eyes.

"Thank you, ma'am." Collette hesitated, then turned and threw the towel overboard. Gradually the towel soaked into the water. Collette turned and gave Elizabeth a quick hug. "I'll be leaving you now. You're a kind woman. What's your name, honey?"

"Elizabeth...Elizabeth Breckenridge."

Collette nodded, then turned and left. Elizabeth felt confused by why Collette would live the way she did if she believed in God. She realized she had so much to learn about real people and real life.

She breathed deeply of the morning air and looked up at the sky. It was then she saw him...Clint Brady... watching her. Surely he'd seen her with Collette. What was he thinking? And why did she have this feeling that

he was *always* watching her? He gave her a smile and a
nod and turned away.

Elizabeth looked back out over the ocean. She could no
longer see the towel, and it struck her that just as that tiny
bit of life was now in God's hands, so was hers. *"Lord, just
don't send me more than I can handle,"* she murmured.
"But I do have so much to learn. Just show me the way."

Chapter Six

> *Beloved, let us love one another: for love is of God; and every one that loveth is born of God, and knoweth God.*
>
> —1 John 4:7

Seattle, August 11, 1898

Elizabeth stood beside the railing of the *Damsel*'s main deck watching supplies being unloaded and a very few passengers disembark at Seattle. Even more men and supplies waited at the dock to board. Among those leaving the steamer were Tricia, Francine and Collette, who stopped at Elizabeth's side for a moment before leaving the ship.

Collette wore a rather plain dress, but it was cut low enough to show sinful cleavage. "We're going to find a doctor for Francine," she told Elizabeth.

Elizabeth glanced at Francine, astonished at how young she, too, looked—as well as how pale, with dark circles under her eyes. "I hope you feel better soon," she told the girl.

Francine nodded a thank-you and looked away, covering her head with a shawl. She left with Tricia, the only one of the three who appeared to be perhaps as old as thirty.

Collette patted Elizabeth's arm. "Francine truly appreciates you praying over that poor little piece of life, and praying for her, too. I hope you don't think too dreadfully of her. She's had a hard life—never knew her father, and her alcoholic mother abandoned her when she was only ten. Her stepfather treated her…well…not like a daughter, that's for sure, if you know what I mean."

Elizabeth thought a moment, feeling ill when she deduced what the woman was trying to tell her. "Oh, how awful!"

"Well, honey, I don't mean to upset you. I just thought maybe it would help for you to understand how some people end up the way they do. Say, how far into Alaska are you headed, anyway?"

Elizabeth's emotions reeled with pity and shock, and she swallowed before replying. "Uh…Dawson—really it's not Alaska at all—it's up in the Yukon."

"Oh, we know where it is. That's where we were headed. Hey, maybe we'll see you up there!"

Elizabeth wasn't so sure she should be glad about that. "Yes, maybe you will. My brother is building a church there, and I'm going to Dawson to join Peter and help him with his ministry."

"Really?" Collette looked her over. "Well, why am I not surprised? You're such a nice, gracious young woman. By gosh, maybe we'll find that church and go there—that is, if your brother would allow it."

Elizabeth smiled, unable not to like the woman in spite

of her occupation. "He would never turn anyone away for any reason. He's a lot like our father, who accepted all people. He was...killed while ministering along the Barbary Coast. His name was William Breckenridge. Perhaps you've heard of him?"

Collette frowned. "Could have. I mean, I remember hearing about some preacher being killed." She shook her head. "I'm real sorry to hear that, Miss Breckenridge. And I hope you have a safe trip to Dawson, but you should know how dangerous it is for you to be doing this alone. The girls and I would have gladly watched out for you, but we'll be taking a different steamer the rest of the way now." She glanced toward the upper deck. "Then again, I have a feeling somebody is already watching out for you."

Elizabeth glanced in the direction where Collette looked, and there stood Clint Brady. She reddened and looked back at Collette. "I don't even know that man. I mean...he helped chase down a man who'd stolen my handbag, but that's the extent of it."

"Well, the girls and I saw the whole thing. We talked to him briefly the day we all boarded the *Damsel*, and he told us about how you were traveling alone and that it worried him."

"Why? He doesn't even know me."

Collette shrugged. "I expect he's just the kind of man who hates thieves and the like—kind of a lawman at heart. He's a bounty hunter, you know."

Elizabeth's eyes widened. "What?"

"That's right. He showed us a drawing of the man he's after, wanted to know if we'd seen him around San Francisco before we left. He's pretty darn sure the man is headed for Dawson, since that's where he's from. So, your Mr. Brady is going there to find him. There's five thousand dollars on his head. Heck, it's probably a quicker way of making five thousand bucks than panning for gold in that miserable back country." She chuckled. "Anyway, he's obviously a man who knows how to handle himself, so if he's got an eye on you, that's good." Collette leaned closer. "And your Mr. Clint Brady is just about the most handsome specimen of man I've ever set eyes on." She winked. "And I've set eyes on plenty!" She laughed then. "I wouldn't be too quick to turn down his attention, sweetie!" She gave Elizabeth a quick hug. "You have a safe trip now."

The woman turned and walked away, and a rather stunned Elizabeth watched after her. Again her thoughts whirled with indecision about people and God's love and what the Lord expected of her. Was he throwing these people at her to teach her something? Thieves. Prostitutes. A bounty hunter! Didn't bounty hunters search out men and kill them for money? What if the men they looked for were innocent? And even if they were guilty of whatever crimes they were accused of, what gave another man the right to pass judgment to the extent of shooting them down without a trial? How could one man treat another man no better than an animal, killing them as they would kill a beaver for its pelt?

No wonder Clint Brady had been unconcerned about whether the man who'd attacked her got out of the water! What would compel a man to have such little concern for human life? She watched the swarm of people on the docks. From what she could tell, she just might.be the only woman on the *Damsel* for the rest of the journey.

She drew a deep breath for courage. So be it. In spite of what she now knew about Clint Brady, she couldn't help hoping, deep inside, that he really would look out for her.

Lord, what would compel such a nice-looking man who apparently cares about other people to be able to kill another human being for money? Have You brought Clint Brady into my life for a reason? How on earth can I be of any help to such a man?

She watched Tricia, Francine and Collette hail a horse-drawn cab and climb inside. Had she been of any help to them? Any influence? "God be with them," she muttered. She looked around, catching a glimpse of Clint Brady talking to some other men. He was showing them something, most likely the drawing of the man he was hunting. "And be with Mr. Brady," she added.

Chapter Seven

Jesus saith unto him, I am the way, the truth and
the life: no man cometh unto the Father, but by me.
—St. John 14:6

Where heaven begins. That was how Peter had described
this land, and Elizabeth was beginning to see what he meant
as the *Damsel* chugged past some of the most magnificent
scenery Elizabeth had ever seen. Because of the stale stench
below deck, she'd spent most of the past three days above
watching the landscape, often pulling her cape close around
her against the cool, misty air. The weather had become
totally unpredictable as the steamer moved through fjords
bordered by mountainous islands that appeared to have no
beaches. It looked as though the deeply forested slopes
simply rose from the sea straight upward.

The mornings were chilly, often followed by a very
warm midday as the sun appeared through the mist, and
yet it could rain within minutes of sunshine, followed by

bright sun again. Every day it rained in spurts, and she had to keep an umbrella with her at all times.

Most of the almost crushing crowd of men on board seemed to have no interest in the gorgeous landscape beyond talk of how much gold lay beneath the distant mountains. She saw a different kind of treasure there, visions of God's beautiful heaven. She realized how right Peter had been in saying that he would be needed at the gold seekers' final destination, for surely there would be hordes of people there who might be hungry for God's Word: people like Collette, who needed to hear about God's forgiveness, men who needed to know that gold was not their God, and men like Clint Brady, who needed their hearts healed by God's love.

Why couldn't she get him off her mind? Why couldn't—

"Miss Breckenridge?"

Elizabeth turned at the words, spoken in a deep voice, Clint Brady's voice. A quick rush of cool air sent a shiver through her, and she drew her cape closer again as she looked up into steel-blue eyes. "Yes?"

He stepped up beside her and leaned on the deck rail. "I have to tell you that I was hoping you'd change your mind and get off at Portland."

Elizabeth frowned in surprise. "Why? You don't even know me. Besides, it's really none of your business where I'm going." She stood next to him, leaning against the railing. Both watched the deep-green mountains as the *Damsel* made its way through currently calm waters.

Clint paused long enough to fiddle with something. Elizabeth waited, not even looking at him, but soon she smelled smoke as he let out a long, deep breath. She glanced at his hands hanging out over the railing, and noticed a cigarette between his fingers.

"Ma'am," he finally spoke up, "I don't think you have an inkling of what you're in for. Even *I* can only guess, from what the rumors are. Either way, it's not an experience for a proper young lady like yourself. A good deal of *men* who make this trip won't manage to even get over the first pass to Dawson. The Canadian North-West Mounted Police are demanding that men tote a good thousand pounds of supplies, because last winter hundreds of men died either trying to get over the passes or from starvation on the way or once they reached Dawson. It's a trip a lot of men can't withstand, let alone a woman alone who doesn't have near the necessary strength to tote a backload of supplies for hundreds of miles. And if that alone isn't enough to make you turn back, you're headed into country where you'll often be caught alone with a pack of men who haven't seen a woman for months. Even the most proper among them would be tempted to forget gentlemanly behavior."

Elizabeth felt a warmth coming into her cheeks at what he was suggesting. "I told you before that God will provide. I trust Him completely, Mr. Brady. Somehow He will help me reach my destination safely."

She heard him give an almost moaning gasp signaling his disbelief. He clearly felt that she was probably stupid and naive to believe what she was saying. He took another long drag on his cigarette.

"Perhaps you don't know much about God and putting your trust in Him, Mr. Brady, but I—"

"Oh, I know all about those things," he interrupted. "I know all too well about trusting God, and how He can completely fail you. Don't preach to me, ma'am. I'm just trying to prevent you from suffering or maybe even losing your life, that's all."

Oh, the bitterness in his comment about God! What was the story behind this man? She remained confused about why he would care about her, and she again asked him that very question.

Clint shifted as though uncomfortable with the entire conversation. "Ma'am, I don't even know why myself. I guess it's because I had a wife once, about your age, and she met with a terrible misfortune. I saw you standing all alone on the dock back in San Francisco and have watched you ever since. I'm worried your simple trust in God is going to make you do something very foolish. It's obvious you aren't very well schooled in life in the real world, and since I don't have much of anything else to do on this journey till I reach Dawson, I figured I'd occupy my time with looking out for you…kind of a leftover from not being there for my wife when she needed me."

So, this had something to do with his wife. Was the life he led also related to what happened to her? She swallowed, not sure just what to say. "Well, Mr. Brady, if you want to go out of your way for me, I suppose I should tell you I appreciate it, but I certainly don't expect it of you or anyone else. It's very kind of you to think of me that way, and I'm deeply sorry for whatever misfortune hurt your wife. Is she well now?"

Another pause, another long drag on the cigarette. "She's dead." The words came flatly, angrily.

"Oh, I'm so very sorry. Truly I am." It was all beginning to make more sense now. Was his wife murdered? Was he searching for her killer?

"I should have made that point in the first place." He sighed and cleared his throat. "I, uh, just want you to know that if you need anything, you can ask. And if I were you, I'd pack some kind of handgun."

Elizabeth had to smile at the very thought of it. "Mr. Brady, that would do me no good. For one thing, I can't afford one, and for another, I wouldn't use it anyway. I could never in my life shoot at someone."

"Not even if they threatened to steal everything you own, or steal what's most precious to you?"

"Most precious?"

She looked up at him curiously. He faced her and rolled his eyes, now appearing rather better-humored. "You don't know what I'm talking about?"

Elizabeth thought a moment, then turned away. "Oh!" She felt ridiculous, embarrassed, angry with him for mentioning such a thing. "God would never allow such a misfortune. Thank you again for your offer, Mr. Brady, but I'll be fine."

He leaned closer. "I meant what I said. Other men might offer the same thing, but I wouldn't trust any of them, understand?"

She drew in her breath, drinking in a bit of courage along with it, and faced him again, hoping her cheeks weren't too flushed. "And why should I trust you and not all the others?"

He looked her over in a way that made her feel safe and warm. It disturbed her to be unable to ignore the fact that he was incredibly handsome. Wasn't it sinful to notice such things about a man?

"Maybe because I'm the one who risked his life to help you out at the docks," he told her. "I didn't see anyone else doing that. Maybe because I've handled some pretty bad characters and know more about that than most of the men on this ship. Maybe because I know how to handle my fists and a gun, which I guarantee you are going to need before this journey ends. And maybe because your God intended for me to notice you. You said yourself that He would be sure you get to Dawson safely. Maybe I'm the reason."

She raised her eyebrows in surprise and grinned. So, he *did* still believe, at least a little. "Are you saying *God* brought us together?"

He gave her a rather sneering smile. "If He did, it was because of you, certainly not because He cares anything about me."

The door was open! "Oh, but He *does*, Mr. Brady. He most certainly does."

Clint took one last drag from his cigarette and tossed the butt into the water. "No, ma'am, I don't think so." He looked around. "Look, there are only three more days left until we reach Skagway. Believe me, when we get there, you'll be thrown into a wide-open, lawless, crowded, wild town where there won't be one man you can trust, and the only women there will be like Collette and those other two who got off at Portland. And, by the way, you need to be careful who you're seen with."

"God loves everyone, Mr. Brady. I can do no less as

His servant. One of them needed my help. I could not turn her away."

He folded his arms, giving her a stern look. "Do you really think that I or the other men on this ship didn't know what was going on?"

Elizabeth's patience was rankled. "It's none of their business, nor yours! They asked me to pray for them, and so I did. I am *not* as naive as you think! My own father was murdered on the Barbary Coast, ministering to harlots and thieves and murderers! I know a little bit about the real world, sir, and I know that *you* are a bounty hunter! You hunt men down for money, so as I said, why should I trust you?"

Why had she said that? She hadn't meant to. She wasn't even going to bring up the subject, which she now knew surely had something to do with his wife! She saw hurt and anger in his eyes. She looked away. "I'm sorry."

"No matter," he said coldly. "I didn't say I was any better than the harlots and murderers you just mentioned. I'm only telling you that I do care what happens to a young woman alone against the odds you'll be facing. In fact, what I was going to say was that for what's left of this journey, you're welcome to use my cabin if you want. I hate to think of you down there with a bunch of men who haven't bathed since God knows when and who I don't doubt are using language you'd rather not listen to. But then since you're more worldly than I thought, I guess it's not so bad for you. And you wouldn't want to stay in a cabin that's been inhabited by a bounty hunter, now, would you? Enjoy the rest of your trip, Miss Breckenridge."

He left her then, and Elizabeth wanted to kick herself.

He'd given her an opening to help him learn about God's love, and she'd missed it! She'd let her own pride and orneriness get in the way. She leaned over the railing again, putting her head in her hands.

Oh, Lord, forgive me! I failed You miserably! Clint Brady had offered to help her, protect her, give up expensive quarters for her, and she'd behaved abominably. What a fool she was! And what a poor servant of the Lord!

Chapter Eight

He that is of God heareth God's words:
ye therefore hear them not, because
ye are not of God.

— St. John 8:47

Clint felt frustrated, angry, anxious, guilty, worried and bored. He tried to think of one positive thing about his life, and he couldn't come up with anything…except Elizabeth Breckenridge, which seemed pretty ridiculous, considering he'd known her all of ten days. Most of that was by sight alone, and the one and only real conversation he'd had with her ended disastrously.

Why in heck did she get to him the way she did? He was making this trip for one reason alone—to find Roland Fisher and either take him back to San Francisco alive, or return with a notarized certificate of his death…by a bullet from Clint Brady's gun. It made no difference to him which way it was. The man was a murderer of innocent people, which meant his life had no value.

The intrusion of Elizabeth Breckenridge into his thoughts and emotions was an unexpected infringement on his life and purpose. Why did he allow it to perplex him? There was absolutely no reason for it, and he wished he'd never run after the thief who took her handbag. Maybe then she would have missed the *Damsel* altogether and he wouldn't be in this mess of emotions.

How could a woman be so ridiculously stupid about her decisions? She was apparently just as misguided as her father had been, actually believing that God would watch out for her and see that she reached Dawson safely. The thought was enough to make a man laugh. Sometimes he wanted to, but the thought of what could really happen to the poor girl sobered him.

He lit another cigarette, glad he'd brought plenty along. Pacing around on the *Damsel* was driving him nuts. He couldn't wait to get off and get away from Miss Naive. At least those below ate at a different time from those with cabins, so he didn't have to see her in the dining room, such as it was. He wondered how her stomach was handling the doughy, half-baked biscuits and tough meat the ship's cook served.

At least once they landed at Skagway he could get away from her. If she was so sure she could make it to Dawson all on her own, then let her find out the hard way that God was *not* going to provide! It would serve her right to discover that maybe there was no God at all. She'd find out how crushing it could be to realize that simple faith wasn't enough when it came to the real evils of the world.

And faith in God was also no use when trying to forget the pain of the past, to get over the loss of loved ones. And forgiveness—that was totally impossible. How can a man forgive those who've robbed him of what was most precious in his life? No, forgiveness is for fools, as is faith in a cruel God. What a mean lesson Miss Breckenridge had yet to learn!

Fools! Half the world was made up of fools. Fools like the men on this ship who'd deserted loved ones to look for a treasure most of them would never find. Fools like Elizabeth Breckenridge. Fools like he'd once been, thinking life could be perfectly wonderful and peaceful and full of joy. He'd almost forgotten what true joy was, forgotten how to smile because of love rather than because of bounty money. He wasn't even sure what to do with all the money he'd gradually built up in a bank in San Francisco. The only things he spent money on were a few clothes, tobacco, the horses that would arrive in Skagway ahead of him on a cattle boat and the best Winchester rifle and Colt handgun money could buy.

A group of men toward the *Damsel*'s bow began singing a risqué song about the women of Skagway and the places they liked to stuff gold nuggets. He wondered if poor Elizabeth could hear the filthy words, then chastised himself for caring. He finished his cigarette and walked over to join the singers, laughing at the dirty lyrics. Laughing. Crying inside.

Elizabeth shivered into her cape, surprised at how cold it was today compared to the lovely day yesterday, with sunshine and no wind. She closed her eyes and concentrated on the beauty of the mountains, softly humming a hymn in her attempt to shut out the dirty, suggestive words of the men singing nearby. Finally the singing stopped when a pod of orca whales began following the ship, sometimes jumping high out of the dark, foggy waters in a magnificent display of black and white majesty.

After nearly a half hour of staying close enough to be seen in spite of the fog, they swam off to the distance, disappearing into the mist. Only minutes later their show was replaced by the antics of a huge herd of chattering dolphins that jumped and rolled and played alongside the ship. The comical sight made Elizabeth and others laugh, and it seemed the blue creatures were laughing with them. They reminded Elizabeth of little children.

It felt good to laugh. Elizabeth glanced around to see if Clint Brady might also be watching the dolphins. She saw him standing farther down along the ship's rail, and yes, he, too, was laughing. She whispered a little prayer of thanks to God for creating something so sweet and beautiful that it could make a man like that forget whatever was burdening him and genuinely laugh, if for just a few moments.

She quickly looked away so he wouldn't catch her watching him, for she suspected he'd fast lose his smile if he knew she'd seen him actually enjoying himself. As little as she knew about him so far, she was pretty sure he'd be stubborn about admitting any kind of brief happiness. Mr. Clint Brady was determined to be mad at the world and at God.

The dolphins disappeared as suddenly as they had appeared, and again the ship was shrouded in thick, cold fog. It was unnerving to know there were islands and rocks and other ships all around, as they'd been watching other steamers ahead of and behind them throughout their voyage. In just one more day, so she'd been told, they would make Skagway, and she would be more than happy to get off the *Damsel* and out of the worsening conditions in the lower deck.

"One more day, fellas," a man nearby shouted.

All the talk was of Skagway and White Pass and Chilkoot Pass and the cost of horses and gear and hope that those who'd gone before had "left some of that there gold for us."

In the distance she could hear another ship's steam whistle. The *Damsel* sounded her own wail in reply, the steam pouring from her stacks only adding to the denseness of the fog. Something about the thick mist made the whistles seem louder than normal, and the other ships' haunting horns seemed all too close.

Suddenly Elizabeth could barely see past her hand, couldn't even see those standing next to her.

How close were other boats? They were in fairly narrow fjords now, no room for error. *"God, protect us,"* she whispered. She'd no more said the words than she felt a jolt, and in what seemed no more than a second she felt the rail on which she leaned give way. She was falling…falling…

She hit the icy water, and the weight of her leather shoes and many layers of under slips, her dress and her fur cape…all caused her to sink…sink…ever deeper.

Chapter Nine

And Jesus said unto him, Receive thy sight:
thy faith hath saved thee.

—St. Luke 18:42

"*Lizzy.*"

Mama?

Elizabeth was sure she'd heard her mother calling her. No one else ever referred to her as Lizzy. She searched the dark waters. Nothing. Was her mother calling her home to heaven? Should she allow her lungs to give up and just breathe in the icy water, allowing herself to drown?

"The Father is with you," her mother told her.

Something strong bumped her, then grabbed her, lifted her. She was near the point of passing out from holding her breath, and from futile efforts to bring herself back to the water's surface. She felt herself rising, rising now instead of sinking. Someone had found her! Who? How many others had fallen overboard when the railing broke?

Thank you, Jesus!

In the next moment her head broke above water and she gasped, desperately gulping air, blessed air. She was alive!

"Hang on to me!" a man's voice commanded.

She obeyed, still not even aware of who it was. He clung to her with one arm and used his other arm to swim.

"Kick your feet a little," he told her.

"I can't swim!"

"Just kick your feet the best you can."

This time the words were shouted. She obeyed, surprised that kicking her feet actually helped. She dug into a muscled back with her right hand as she clung to whoever held her. "Don't let go!" she found herself begging, her words coming through chattering teeth.

The arm holding her tightened. "I didn't jump into this ice bath just to let go of you after finding you," he shouted in reply.

Clint? It sounded like Clint Brady! Had he also fallen in from the broken railing, or had he deliberately dived in after her? Those thoughts flickered through her brain as she struggled against the cruel cold of the water and kept kicking in spite of the weight of her dress and shoes. Between the heavy fog and the water splashing into her eyes, she could barely see a thing, including the man rescuing her. A small boat appeared out of nowhere, and the man led her to it, lifting her slightly.

"Grab on!"

Now Elizabeth could hear other voices, men yelling for help. Two men in the boat reached for her, and the man who'd helped her put his hand on her rump and gave her a boost. She managed to climb over the side of the smaller boat and literally fall into it.

"Hello!" one of the men in the boat shouted. "We're here! We've got a boat. Swim toward our voices."

Coughing and shivering, Elizabeth managed to sit up and stare over the side of the boat. What had happened to Clint?

"You'll be okay now, ma'am," one of those in the boat told her. "We got rammed by another steamer, but the *Damsel* will make it to the closest island. We'll get help right quick, and we'll still make it to Skagway."

Breathless, Elizabeth couldn't even answer. She recognized the man as one of the *Damsel*'s crew. Another man removed his pea coat and put it around her shoulders. Elizabeth very gladly pulled it closer, wondering if she would ever feel warm again. She continued gasping as she waited, watching for Clint to emerge.

After a few minutes two more men came to the side of the boat. To her relief she could see Clint was one of them. The fog seemed to be lifting slightly, enough that she realized Clint had gone out to save someone else. He helped the man to the boat and left yet again, seemingly immune to the cold water.

Minutes later he again returned with yet another man. This time he climbed inside after the man he'd helped. He fell to the bottom of the boat, breathing hard, and Elizabeth noticed he wore only a shirt and pants—no jacket, no gun and no boots or even socks! Surely he hadn't fallen in accidentally at all. He'd taken a moment to half undress so he could swim better, having every intention of rescuing as many as he could.

He sat up and put his head in his hands, still breathing deeply, and there came another cry for help, somewhere in the fog. Clint stood up and dove off the small boat again.

"Clint!" Elizabeth screamed.

Moments later he returned with a third man. Both of them climbed into the boat.

"I hope…that's all of them," Clint panted.

"It's a mighty fine thing you did, mister," one of the crewmen told him.

"Where did you learn to swim so good?" one of those he'd rescued asked.

"Lake Michigan," Clint answered, "a long time ago. I wasn't so sure I'd have the strength I needed, it's been so long." He took several more deep breaths. "Good thing I got the last of you. I was about out of breath." He coughed and glanced at Elizabeth. "You all right?"

"I think so. Oh, Clint, how can I thank you enough? First my handbag, now this—"

"Don't worry about it," he waved her off. He coughed again, then sneezed. "Let's get back to the *Damsel*," he told one of the crewmen, who began rowing.

The crewmen and others from the ship began shouting back and forth to each other, and in moments the *Damsel*, its back end sitting low in the water, came into sight. Another ship sat close by.

"She's takin' on water, but she'll make it to the closest island," one of the crewmen repeated. Men on board threw down ropes, and the crewmen rigged them to trollies on each end of the smaller boat, tossing the ends back up to the deck, where men began hauling the lifeboat upward in even jerks until it was high enough for the passengers to climb onto the deck.

Clint helped lift Elizabeth, and she couldn't help being aware of his strength. Men on deck helped her the rest of the way up, then helped Clint climb on deck. Those he'd rescued were already telling others what Clint had done and what a good swimmer he was. There came a round of thank-yous, and Clint took Elizabeth's arm.

"You're coming to my cabin whether you want to or not. No arguments! You're getting out of those wet clothes and under some covers, and then you're going to pray you don't get sick."

The words were spoken with such command that Elizabeth didn't even consider arguing. She had to half run to keep up with him as he directed her to the wooden steps that led to cabins on the second level. She lifted her soaked dress and managed to climb the stairs, feeling more and more weary with every step, worn out from her struggle, shivering fiercely from the cold. She followed Clint through a door.

"What about the steamer? Isn't it sinking?" she asked Clint.

"They said we'd get to the closest island, and I believe them. Other ships will come along to help us. They'll figure it out." Clint closed the door. "Meantime, we're on the second level. We can probably stay right here until help arrives."

We? "I…what will I change into? What about my things below?"

"I'll go get them for you. You get yourself undressed and under those covers."

"But…I don't have anything to wear!"

Looking rather disgusted, Clint dug through a duffel bag and threw a shirt at her. "Put this on and just get under the covers. I'll be back."

Still soaked and shivering himself, he left before Elizabeth could say a thing. She looked around the tiny room, lit by a lantern and warmed by a small, potbelly stove. She could see glowing embers through the partially open vent. She felt totally bewildered, full of questions, as she began undressing.

Realizing Clint could come back any time, Elizabeth hastily removed her dress, her many slips, her now-squishy high-button shoes, her stockings, and her camisole. Her money fell out. She gasped and quickly gathered it up, looking around for a place to put it, then turned and shoved it under the feather mattress of Clint's narrow bed.

She then removed her wet drawers. "Oh, dear Lord!" she lamented. She was completely naked, but how else was she to dry off and get warm? Still, she was in a man's cabin, about to crawl into a man's bed! How humiliating!

She hurriedly put on the shirt he'd given her, which was far too big. It fell past her knees, but as far as she was concerned, it still didn't cover her legs enough. Elizabeth looked around again, noticing Clint's six-gun hanging over the back of a wooden chair, looking so intimidating and dangerous. She noticed a towel lying beside a bowl and pitcher, and she grabbed it up to dry her hair as best she could, taking out the few pins left in it.

Suddenly she felt nauseated and dizzy. She crawled under the covers, pulling them over herself and settled into the pillow, relishing the warmth of the room, the comfort of the first bed she'd slept in for over a week. She could smell Clint's scent in the pillow, a very pleasant, manly scent, much nicer than the smells below deck. The room itself smelled of cigarettes, leather and wood smoke.

She watched the red coals of the stove, and thought what a blessing fire could be.

"Thank You, Jesus," she whispered, *"for fire, for saving me...for Clint Brady."* Oh, how wonderful felt the warmth of that potbelly stove! She thought about hearing her mother's voice. "Thank you, Mama," she whispered.

Chapter Ten

Fear ye not therefore, ye are of more value than
many sparrows.
—St. Matthew 10:31

Elizabeth stirred, for a brief moment remembering lying
in bed at home in San Francisco, the smell of bacon
cooking downstairs, knowing her mother was in the
kitchen preparing breakfast. She loved those moments, the
peace, the feeling of love and safety.

In seconds she came fully awake, realizing she was not
in her own bed at home at all and gradually remembering
where she really was. She lay still a moment, blinking open
her eyes to see through the porthole in the steel door of the
cabin. It was light out. How long had she slept? She turned
over, at first watching a small fire in the potbelly stove, then
realizing through the bit of light that came through the
porthole that a man was sitting on the floor near the stove,
quietly smoking. He had long legs and wore denim pants.

It was only then that she became fully aware of where she was and what had happened. She jerked the blankets to her neck. She put a hand to her hair, realizing it was entirely undone.

"Good morning," came Clint's low voice.

Elizabeth thought a moment. Morning? The accident had happened midmorning. Had she slept such a short while? "I...good morning," she answered, feeling embarrassed and awkward. "What time is it?"

He took a long drag on his cigarette, then reached over and flicked it through the slats of the wood burner. "About nine-thirty."

Elizabeth frowned. Nine-thirty? "But...it was later than that when I fell overboard."

"Yup." Clint sneezed before continuing. "About twenty-two hours ago."

"What! You mean it's the next *day?*"

"Yes, ma'am. You've had a right good sleep."

Astounded, Elizabeth put her hand to her mouth. "I don't believe it!"

Clint stretched, sneezed again, excused himself. "Well, it's true. We've been stranded here since the accident. They're hoping to load some of the passengers onto the next ship that comes by, then more on the next and so forth, till we're all off and on our way to Skagway. We ought to be able to get off later today and make Skagway by tomorrow morning."

Elizabeth rolled to her back and stared at the ceiling. "Oh, I'm so embarrassed, and so sorry! Where on earth did *you* sleep last night?"

"Outside under the stars. Doesn't bother me much. I've spent plenty of nights sleeping on the hard ground with a saddle for a pillow. I just now came in to get warm."

Elizabeth struggled to untangle her thoughts. She pulled the blankets clear up to her nose. "This is terrible. I'm so sorry, and so embarrassed."

"You already said that, and I have no idea why you think that way."

"But I've put you out…and what must the other men think, me sleeping here in your cabin."

He sneezed yet again, then cleared his throat. "They can think what they want. Besides, most of them are only concerned with how soon they can get on another ship and get themselves to Skagway. They're all pretty upset that they've had a setback, all anxious to get to their gold. I can tell you right now that most of them won't find any. I can think of a lot of ways to make good money a lot faster and with less discomfort."

By killing wanted men? She wanted to ask.

Clint leaned forward and rubbed at the back of his neck, squinting slightly as though in pain. Then he sneezed again.

"Are you catching a cold, Mr. Brady?"

He reached toward a saddle bag and pulled out a hand-kerchief. "I'll be all right."

She watched him quietly a moment. "You could get very sick, after what you did yesterday. Those men and I owe you a lot, me especially. That's the second time you've helped me." Her throat swelled with a sudden urge to cry. "I was so sure I was going to die. How can I ever, ever thank you enough?"

He shrugged. "I just reacted. I used to be a pretty good swimmer." He leaned his head back against the wall.

"I think I remember you saying something about Lake Michigan to someone. Is that where you learned to swim?"

He waited a moment to answer. "I was a kid," he finally told her. "I grew up near Chicago. Then my folks got tired of city life and moved to Nebraska to farm. My mother died when I was seventeen, my father the next year, which left me on my own. I didn't much like the humidity and the mosquitoes in that part of the country, so I headed for California. I'd heard others talk about how nice it was there."

Elizabeth listened to the sound of heated wood snapping and popping in the stove. It relaxed her. "My parents came west from Illinois, too, only farther south from Chicago. I never got to see the Great Lakes. Are they as big and beautiful as I've heard?"

He drew a deep breath. "From what I can remember. It's been years. I do remember that Lake Michigan was so big that you couldn't see the other side of it. Big ships, much bigger than this steamer, would dock in Chicago, bringing goods from practically all over the world, mostly from Europe and, of course, from places like Boston and New York City." He rubbed at his eyes. "But that was a long time ago. Chicago is probably all changed and a heck of a lot bigger by now."

"I'm sorry about your parents. It must have been hard for you. It sounds like you had no brothers or sisters."

"Neither one." The air hung quiet for a moment. "I still miss them sometimes. They were good Christian people." He sneezed again and kept rubbing at his eyes.

Elizabeth was surprised at his reference to "good Christian people." This man apparently had had a Christian upbringing. What on earth had turned him to the life he led now? Youthful curiosity left her dying to ask, but good manners meant not prying into other people's business, especially not a man she suspected gave such information only when good and ready.

"I'm sorry you're not feeling well," she told him. "If you will leave for a while I'll get dressed, you can have your bed back." Privately she thought how wonderful it would feel to stay in the bed all day. "And again I'm sorry to take it from you for so long. I must have been far more exhausted than I thought. All the time I've been on this boat I've barely slept for all the noise and stench below, and worrying about someone trying to rob me. And then nearly drowning yesterday…" Again she remembered her mother calling to her. "My mother's sweet spirit must be very strong."

Clint frowned. "What do you mean?"

Elizabeth turned on her side and curled up. "She called to me. She's the reason you jumped into the water, you know…my mother…and God."

He grunted a laugh. "They were, were they?"

"I'm serious, Mr. Brady. They used you to help me."

He simply chuckled wryly and shook his head.

"You don't believe in the spirits of dead loved ones being able to reach out to you?"

He took several long seconds to answer. "Maybe… sometimes." Again he sneezed. He took a moment to blow his nose. "I'm surprised you believe in such things. Isn't it anti-Christian to believe in spirits?"

"Oh, on the contrary. For one thing, we don't really die anyway, not those who truly have loved and served God. We just travel heaven's pathway to a beautiful home filled with peace and flowers and the glory of God. I like to believe that since our spirits simply take on a new form and live on with God, He allows us to hover close to our loved ones still living on earth and to help them however we can. God surely has enough to do. I believe He uses our spirits to help Him with His constant vigil to protect and love His children on earth."

He shook his head again, grunting a little as he stood up and stretched. "Well, I don't see where He does a very good job of protecting those still on earth. And me managing to find you like I did was just a quirk—nothing special."

She smiled softly. "You don't really believe that. The other men you helped were thrashing and yelling, easier to find. But me, I was sinking far below the surface, yet you found me. No one could ever convince me that God and my mother didn't have something to do with that."

Clint rummaged in one of his own carpet bags and pulled out yet another clean shirt. He began unbuttoning the one he wore, and Elizabeth's eyes widened when she realized he was going to take it off in front of her! Other than black men working on the wharf in San Francisco, she'd never seen a man with his shirt off! She pulled the blankets over her head. "Mr. Brady!"

"What?"

"Couldn't you wait until I'm gone to change your shirt?"

This time his light laughter sounded genuine. "You've never seen a man with his shirt off?"

"Of course not!"

"Not even your father or your brother?"

"Heavens no!"

Elizabeth heard the soft rustle of clothes. "Lady, your situation is even worse than I thought."

Elizabeth waited, refusing to uncover her eyes.

"You can look now," he finally told her.

Slowly she pulled the covers away to see him wearing a shirt and a leather vest. He was leaning over pulling on socks and boots.

"I think these boots have dried out," he told her as he finished dressing. "By the way, in case you didn't notice, I brought your things up from below, and I laid your wet clothes around the room to dry out." He sneezed again. "I'll leave for a while and you can dress and go to the kitchen and get something to eat, such as it is. At least you can get some hot coffee. You might as well pack up as best you can and be prepared to leave the ship later today. Next stop is Skagway. It's a good thing you got some rest. You'll need it when you reach that town. Rough and lawless, they say." He straightened. "Did your money survive?"

"Yes, it's under your mattress."

He grinned and shook his head again. "Don't tell me you thought I'd *steal* it."

"Well, I…I just wasn't sure where to put it."

He chuckled. "Just make sure you stuff it back into your camisole." He winked. "Where it's dang sure safe."

He walked out the door, and Elizabeth wanted to crawl through the cracks in the floors and disappear. She looked around the room to see that Clint had indeed hung her clothes all about the cabin to dry—including her camisole, under slips and drawers!

She closed her eyes in humiliation.

Chapter Eleven

*For now we see through a glass, darkly; but then
face to face: Now I know in part; but then shall I
know even as also I am known.*
                                        —1 Corinthians 13:12

Skagway, August 20, 1898

Clint could see the outline of Skagway in the distance, visible only because of smoke and steam from the stacks of other steamers docked there. The crew of the *Damsel* had managed to keep the steamer's leak in check enough to bring the ship into the "jumping-off" town with the help of a tugboat sent from there. That meant that everyone on board the *Damsel* could stay there and be towed in, much to the chagrin of some who were bent on getting to the town a day sooner.

Clint wouldn't have minded if not for the fact that waiting the extra day had meant letting Elizabeth Breckenridge sleep in his cabin one more night. Try as he might, he couldn't get the picture of her in his bed out of his mind.

If ever his resolve to resist temptation had been tested to the limit, the last two nights had been it. He'd managed until now not to think about how long it had been since he'd been with a woman. After Jenny was killed, all desire for any other woman in his life had left him. After a matter of time, he'd not even cared about being with easy women, let alone giving one thought to truly having feelings for any woman ever again.

So why had Elizabeth Breckenridge changed all that? It made him so angry he could spit. This was never supposed to happen to him again. For one thing, it was dangerous to care. That meant risking having his heart shattered yet again, and it wasn't even mended from the first disaster. Besides that, he was full of too much hatred and anger to find room for caring about anyone. He hadn't even cared about himself for the past four years. How many times had he wished that in pursuit of a criminal he'd get shot and killed so the pain in his heart would go away forever? Then he could be with Jenny... and little Ethan.

There came the sharp pain again, so real that it made him grasp the rail and bend over. For months now he'd managed to stop thinking about his son altogether. Maybe, just maybe, he could have gotten over Jenny, if only he still had his little boy...his sweet, innocent, joyful little blue-eyed, blond-haired son named after his daddy. From the day he'd had to look at that beautiful child lying dead he'd never again used his real first name, because every time someone would call him Ethan he'd think about that baby. He used only his middle name now. That helped some.

A hard sneeze brought him out of the pain of the past long enough to remember how lousy he felt today. This was the worst cold he'd ever experienced, and it hadn't helped sleeping on the deck last night. It had rained, as it seemed to do several times a day in this place, but at night it was a cold rain that went to the bone. He'd covered himself with a tarp, but the dampness had enveloped him anyway. Every bone and muscle in his body ached. It hurt to breathe, hurt even more to cough, hurt to look at bright light, hurt to move at all.

As soon as he reached Skagway he hoped to find one available hotel room where he could stay in bed for a day or two before heading into God-knew-what in his effort to reach Dawson. He could only hope that the holdup wouldn't mean missing his chance to corral Roland Fisher. If he somehow heard Clint was after him, he might slip away.

Life sure had taken a strange turn since he'd first tackled the man who stole Elizabeth's handbag. Something about this whole trip just didn't seem right, kind of like he suddenly was not in full control of his life. Elizabeth weighed on his mind like an anvil, and try as he might, he couldn't keep from feeling like he should watch out for her. He thought he'd be glad to reach Skagway, where he could let her go her own way. If that meant she'd really be dumb enough to try to reach Dawson this late in the year, then so be it. And yet the thought of it drove him nuts. How could he let her try to do that alone? Stupid as the idea was, he had to admire her gumption…and her unending faith that God would help her.

At the same time, he couldn't help feeling sorry for her having that faith. God would find a way to shatter it, just as his own faith had been shattered. Fact was, he hadn't even given much thought to God for the past four years, until Miss High-and-Mighty-Holy-Roller had come along, constantly throwing God in his face. There again, he had no control over having to listen to her rhetoric about God and Jesus and prayer and all that bunk. That's what made it so senseless to think about helping her get to Dawson, which was exactly what he'd been thinking about doing…probably the worst decision he could possibly make.

Another sneeze. Could a man feel any worse than this without being dead?

"Clint?"

Someone touched his arm. Naturally it was Elizabeth.

"You're even sicker, aren't you? I'm so sorry you had to sleep on the deck last night. I told you I'd gladly go back below."

He sneezed again, which only increased his irritation with her and then enhanced his anger with himself for *being* irritated with her, because the way he was feeling inside wasn't her fault. It was his own. Still, that didn't stop his sharp retort. "I wish you'd stop bringing it up. I told you that you could have the bed and that's that." He sneezed, and she leaned closer to study him as he blew his sore nose.

"Oh, you poor man. You look awful!"

"Gee, thanks." He coughed, his chest so sore that he hadn't even craved a cigarette.

"I hope you will see a doctor when we reach Skagway."

"I don't need one. I just need a day or two of rest. I'll be fine."

"I wish there was something I could do. You've done so much for me."

"I'll get over it."

"Well, I think you should definitely see a doctor."

"Will you just leave it alone? I'll be all right." He knew she was right about one thing. He must look terrible. He kept his handkerchief over his nose so she couldn't see how red it was. He leaned over the railing again, looking away from her as the outline of Skagway came ever closer. Other men on deck were getting excited, some whooping and hollering at the sight of their jumping-off point. He heard Elizabeth take a deep breath, for courage, he suspected.

"I guess this is it," she told him. "I hope you stay in Skagway and rest up a bit before you go on, and I will pray for your health and for a safe trip."

"Pray for yourself. You're the one who will need help, not me."

Another sigh. "If you are so adamant that it was all right that I use your cabin again last night, Mr. Brady, then please stop being so angry and making me feel so guilty about it."

How he wished that she would just magically drop out of his life. "Sorry. I just feel rotten, that's all." He sneezed again. "I am not in the mood for small talk." He blew his nose and finally looked at her again. She looked as pretty as ever, and it irked him that he'd taken a cold and she seemed to be just fine. Wasn't the man supposed to be the stronger one? How humiliating! He hated showing any kind of weakness.

"Well, then, I'm sorry I bothered you," she answered, looking almost ready to cry. "I just wanted to let you know that I have everything out of your cabin. Once we reach Skagway we might not see each other again, so I just…I truly, truly am grateful, Mr. Brady, for everything you've done for me, and for being so kind as to let me have your cabin the last two nights. You're a good man at heart. Anyone can see that. I will pray that whatever is eating you up on the inside, God will bless you with a way to overcome the pain and be happy again. And I pray that you will be able to stop doing what you do for money. God will forgive you, you know, because only He understands why you do it. I just wanted to tell you that He loves you and—"

Clint rolled his eyes. "Thank you, but save the sermon. I hope the best for you, too. And I still advise you to get yourself a handgun, and be very, very careful who you trust. Find someone to travel with, preferably a man who is taking his wife along so you'll be with another woman." He sneezed. "Good luck, Elizabeth. You'll need it," he said as he moved away.

The *Damsel* let off three loud whistles then, as the tugboat hauled her even closer. Skagway was very visible now, and her docks were crowded with men who'd just disembarked from another steamer that had arrived ahead of them. The men on the *Damsel* began getting even more excited, shouting about gold and land and women and whiskey and dogs and horses and sleds and the best route to take for Dawson. They pushed and shoved to get a better look, some of them forcing Elizabeth away from the railing.

Clint looked back to see her watching him with tears in her eyes. She had to be scared to death. He turned away. She'd made her decision. He had his own agenda.

Chapter Twelve

*The Lord is my shepherd; I shall not want. He
maketh me to lie down in green pastures:
He leadeth me beside the still waters. He restoreth
my soul…I will fear no evil, for Thou art with me.*
—Psalms 23:1-4

It was all Elizabeth could do to hang on to her bags, there
was so much pushing and shoving to get off the *Damsel*.
Most of those who pushed their way past her seemed
hardly aware she existed. The day had turned sunny and
warm, but because of the constant spurts of rain, she
stepped into mud as soon as her feet hit land.

She had no choice but to follow the crowd and walk past
a literal town of tents on the beach, her shoes sinking into
the damp sand. Men and dogs and supplies were absolutely
everywhere. Stove chimneys stuck up through the tops of
the tents. Stacks of barrels of flour and crates of canned
goods were piled so high it appeared they would surely

topple. Some of the men literally ran toward Skagway's main street, and she had no choice but to go with the flow or be knocked over.

The throng shoved her into the main, muddy street, through slop and horse manure. After a desperate search to get out of the way, she finally spotted an opening to her left that brought her to a boardwalk and directly in front of swinging doors. From the other side she could hear a piano playing, men shouting and women laughing. The smell of whiskey and smoke permeated her nostrils, and she quickly moved away from the doorway. She couldn't help peeking through a window, and her eyes widened at the sight of women dancing on a platform, lifting colorful ruffled skirts to show their legs.

She turned away, feeling guilty for looking in the first place. Still, the sight made her wonder about Collette and her friends. She hoped Francine was all right.

She shook away the thought and hurried on, facing the fact that for the time being she had to look out for herself and not worry about others, including Clint Brady. He'd said something to her yesterday about having to locate three horses he'd sent ahead. He'd been worried about someone making off with his horses, as he'd heard the animals were worth plenty in Skagway. Most men arrived here without them and had to pack their own gear over the passes, which meant constantly backtracking all the way over the passes as the gear often weighed hundreds, even thousands of pounds. Word was, many never even made it over the passes to begin with.

Elizabeth had decided that would not be a problem for

her, as all she intended to take were her bags. She would visit the sawmill and see if perhaps someone there could build her a sled that she could attach to her waist and use to pull her bags and however much food she would have to bring along. That would probably take whatever money she had left, but she certainly wouldn't need any more money before reaching Dawson. Once she was with Peter, she'd be safe and never alone again. Whatever Peter did, wherever he went, she would stay with her brother. She couldn't wait to see him.

Yes, that's what she would concentrate on. She would forget about those poor, lost women, forget about Clint Brady, forget about her own fear of the journey ahead. Collette and her friends were likely not at all concerned with what had happened to her, and Clint Brady had brushed her off like a pesky fly. Why should she care that the man was sick and lonely and wayward? Her attempted words of comfort had only angered him, and he obviously did not want her bothering him any more. So be it.

She put her head down and charged forward, ignoring other people, watching her step as she walked down wooden steps, crossed in front of an alley, walked up more steps to the next block of boardwalk. She looked at every window she passed, and every other establishment seemed to be a saloon. In between were supply stores, attorneys' offices, banks, a newspaper office and finally she came across a hotel. She had to climb even more steps to reach the entrance, and from that standpoint she could see another hotel, a blacksmith's barn, more supply stores, a sign that read Boats, another that read Book Store, and a few restaurants. The words Saloon and Bank far outnumbered all others.

Above some of the saloons were balconies upon which stood brightly dressed women, many of whom wore dresses cut so low that they barely covered the merchandise being advertised. She noticed one woman who wore only underclothes. She was laughing and waving at the throng of men in the street.

The sight was difficult to believe. Now and again a supply wagon would splatter past, churning up the mud. She smelled the sweet scent of fresh-cut pine, and in the distance she could hear the grinding sounds of the sawmill that created the smell. She recalled someone on the *Damsel* saying something about Skagway being nothing but a couple of buildings just a year ago, then becoming a huge tent city almost overnight. Now most of the tents had become real buildings, and more building was continuing. The air rang with the pounding of hammers and the scraping of saws and was redolent with the smell of fresh lumber.

Smoke rose into the air from a hundred sources, mostly from the stacks of the steamers at the shoreline and from wood-burning stoves inside most of the buildings. Elizabeth could not help thinking what rich men the suppliers must be, and those who made wood stoves and guns and shovels and boots and the like. She thought how, if she were not alone and unsure of what to do next, this could be terribly exciting. As big as San Francisco was now, she had never seen so many people crowded together in one small place, or heard so much noise or seen so much bustle and commotion. She imagined San Francisco must have been like this during the gold rush in California, but that had taken place long before she was born.

Without even realizing it, she found herself scanning the throngs of men for one face. Tall as he was, Clint Brady would surely be easy to find. He usually wore a leather vest and a wide-brimmed, Western hat, different from the wool felt derbys most men wore, whether dressed in suits or in more rugged clothing.

She searched patiently, but caught no glimpse of Clint. Then she rolled her eyes in disgust with herself for wanting to find him. She'd just convinced herself it was stupid to look, and even though God surely intended for her to help him in some way, there was nothing she could do if he was determined to keep her out of his life.

She turned and picked up her bags, going into the hotel. It had been a long day, and she felt literally banged up from struggling through the crowd to get this far. She walked across a plank floor to greet the desk clerk. "Might I be lucky enough to find a room for the night?" she asked.

The very short, bespectacled man frowned. "I'm very sorry, lady, but I'm full up."

Elizabeth's heart fell. "Is there *any* hotel in town that might have room?"

The man pursed thin lips and thought. "Well, you seem like a nice young lady, and I know for a fact you won't find a room anyplace else, either. I hate to put you out." He looked past her. "Did your husband bring a tent along or something like that?"

She hated telling a stranger that she was alone. "I'm...I don't have a husband, but my brother is meeting me in town from a different boat in a few days. I really need a place to stay in the meantime. I'll take anything. It doesn't have to be fancy."

He rubbed his forehead, then ran a hand through thinning hair. "Well, my own wife would be real upset if I sent you back into the streets without shelter." He leaned closer. "Don't tell anybody, but I can let you stay in a storeroom in the back. I can set up a cot in there, and there's a wash bowl and pitcher, and a privy just outside the back door. It's the best I can do. I'd have to charge you fifty cents."

Elizabeth breathed a sigh of relief. "That will do fine!" It was a relief to actually find a kind man who was truly concerned about her well-being. His smile was warm and genuine. Yes, God was looking out for her after all!

She dug into her handbag for some of the loose change and smaller bills she kept in it and dug out the required fee. "As far as I know it will only be one night, but is it all right if I let you know tomorrow if I find I need a second night's stay?"

"Sure thing. Fact is, by then one of my roomers might leave and you can have his room."

"Oh, thank you!"

The clerk turned the registration book around so she could sign it. "Awfully wild and raw place for a nice lady like yourself," he told her as she dipped the pen into an inkwell and signed her name.

"A person just does what she has to do sometimes, Mr.— Oh, what is your name?"

"Michael Wheeler, ma'am. Wife and I came here last summer from Seattle—figured we'd make more money putting people up than looking for gold, so we sold everything and came here to build this hotel. Don't serve any food, I'm afraid. You'll have to go out for that. I can bring you an extra pitcher of water for drinking, though."

"That would be wonderful."

Wheeler closed the book and signaled for her to follow him. He led her to a room behind his office, where stacks of blankets and pillows and towels were stored, as well as a few brooms, crates of soap bars, several oil lamps, a box of ink jars, several books and ledgers and a few extra bowls and pitchers.

"The wife and I live in an apartment in back of the second-floor rooms," the man told her. "Right now we only have ten rooms, but we plan to add on a third floor and expand the first two."

"Well, I'm glad you're doing so well," Elizabeth told him.

"There's a bolt lock right here on your side of the doorway, and the back door there, it has one, too, so once you're down for the night, just slip both locks closed and you'll be plenty safe. Me or the wife might end up knocking on the door to get something, but that almost never happens once everybody is bedded down for the night. Trouble is, this is a town that never sleeps, if you know what I mean, so you're better off back here anyway. You won't hear the noise from the streets near as bad back here."

"Thank you so much. You're very kind. Perhaps in the morning you can advise me on what things I'll need to journey to Dawson."

The man's smile faded. "*Dawson?* You're headed for *Dawson?*" He spoke the words as though she was insane.

"Yes." She remembered the story she'd told him about

her brother. "As soon as my brother arrives, we'll go together. I just thought I'd get a head start on supplies."

Wheeler shook his head. "Ma'am, brother or not, I wouldn't advise you to head for Dawson till next spring. I mean, I know a lot of the new arrivals here are headed that way, but they're men and they're determined to find gold. Most of them are going to regret leaving this late in the year. But…I mean…men can take care of themselves, you know? And maybe your brother can, too, but he ought not to take you along. You should wait and leave next spring. It's a rough trip, miss, a real rough trip. A lot of the men headed there will never make it."

His words dashed the excitement and affirmation she'd allowed to build within her spirit. Her chest tightened with trepidation. "Nevertheless," she replied, "it's important that I…I mean we…go this year. But thank you for the warning. I'm sure we'll be all right. God is with us, Mr. Wheeler."

He shook his head. "Well, I sure hope so, ma'am. I sure hope so." He shook his head again. "I'll go rummage up a cot for you. There's an extra one in one of the rooms."

Wheeler nodded to her and left, closing the door behind him. Elizabeth drew a deep breath against the sudden urge to cry. She sat down in a wooden chair and put her head in her hands. *"Dear Lord, help me to be strong,"* she prayed. *"Show me the way."*

Chapter Thirteen

For I was an hungered, and ye gave me meat: I
was thirsty, and ye gave me drink: I was a
stranger, and ye took me in: ...I was sick, and ye
visited me.
—St. Matthew 25:35 & 36

Mr. Wheeler was right. Skagway never slept. Even though Elizabeth was at the back of the hotel, she could still hear talking and laughing, sometimes a scream, even gunfire a time or two. More conversation with the hotel's owner enlightened her to the fact that the crowds of men in town were a grand mixture of those planning to head for Dawson and many more who had started the journey and turned back because of the hardships. There were also those who had already been to Dawson and been disappointed to find most good claims had already been laid. And many, like Mr. Wheeler himself, had come to Skagway with the intention of staying put and making their money off the other groups of people. These included the men who owned the saloons and other business establishments, and those who owned the steamers that brought men here and would take many of those same men, and the gold, back to the States.

Tired as she was, Elizabeth lay awake wondering if indeed she should wait until spring to make for Dawson. But what in the world would she do over the winter to survive? Perhaps she could find some kind of work here in Skagway, but this was such a wild town, and she was already tired of being so alone and unsure.

She finally fell into a fitful sleep filled with crazy dreams, the purgatory between asleep and awake. She dreamed that the whole town of Skagway was under water, and she was trying to swim to the top of the hotel. Her mother stood near the chimney, smiling at her. Then Peter floated by in a rowboat that had smokestacks on it, but he didn't stop to pick her up. Collette and her friends sat on the roof of a nearby building laughing at her. One man swam past her and stole her hat. She tried to swim after him, but he was too fast for her. Reverend Selby threw a Bible at her, and she clung to it to stay afloat.

Finally she floated past some steps where a man stood. It was Clint Brady. He smiled and reached for her, and she grabbed his strong arms. He pulled her up, but then he started sneezing and dropped her. Then both of them began coughing, and she began drowning. She cried out for help. Help. Help.

"Help," she murmured in her sleep. In the dream she was screaming the word. She jumped awake, only half aware at first that she'd been trying to cry out in her sleep. She sat up and shook her head, deciding that if she went right back to sleep her brain would return to the silly but stressful dream. Even awake she could swear she still heard Clint coughing.

She stood up, running a hand through her hair and shaking it out, realizing only then that she *was* hearing a man cough. It was a terrible, deep cough, and it came from not far outside her door. Then came the sneezing. It all sounded familiar.

"Clint?" she said softly. It couldn't be. She went to the door that divided the store room from the lobby, then slid the bolt, cracking the door open slightly to peek out. If someone was out there, she didn't want them to see her in her flannel nightgown.

There came the coughing again. A man lay in a bedroll behind the clerk's desk, apparently having been allowed to sleep there for the night. The hotel did not yet have electricity, and by the soft light of a lantern Elizabeth could see he was a big man. Was it Clint? Whoever it was, he sounded very sick. Surely the Lord would want her to see if there was anything she could do for him. He shouldn't be sleeping on a hard, drafty floor.

She quickly turned and pulled on a flannel robe, tying it tightly. She walked into the lobby, looking around to see that no one was there but the sick man. She walked noiselessly over to him and leaned closer.

"Clint!" she said in a half whisper. His breathing was horribly rattled.

"Liz…beth?" he murmured. Immediately he started

coughing again, a cough that made him sit up and lean over. He held his chest and gasped for breath.

Elizabeth dared to reach out and touch his face. "Dear Lord, you're burning up! Clint, you're a terribly sick man! Come into the back room and lie down on my cot. You shouldn't be out here on the floor."

"No...rooms..." he choked out.

"I know. That's why I'm in the storeroom. Please, Clint, let me help you back there. I'll try to find a doctor for you."

"Be...okay..." He coughed again, and his whole body trembled. "Don't want to...put you out."

"After what you did for me? And I wasn't even sick! You will *not* lie out here like this! Please, Clint, come to the back room. It's warmer in there. There is a little wood-burning stove in there that Mr. Wheeler let me use. I'll see if I can find a teakettle back there and heat some water on it. And I'll wake up Mr. Wheeler and see if his wife can lend me some tea. Maybe Mr. Wheeler can send for a doctor."

"No. I can't...let you..." He coughed again. "Never... felt like this...in my life."

"And you *are* going to let me help you, whether you like it or not! If you don't come lie down on my cot I'll find some men to come and *drag* you in there! I swear it!"

Clint groaned again, clinging to his chest as he managed to reach up with his other hand and grab hold of the desk top to pull himself up. Elizabeth put her arm about his waist and let him lean on her. She led him into the back room and ordered him onto her cot, which he seemed to take gladly. She helped him remove his boots and jacket, and he then curled onto the cot, the raspy, deep cough consuming him again as she threw her blankets over him, even though he was still fully dressed.

"Don't you get up from here," she ordered, tucking blankets around his neck. "I'm going for that tea and a doctor!" His condition frightened her. She'd never seen anyone so sick, other than when her mother had died of the ugly cancer. This was different. She knew that sometimes people died from pneumonia, and surely that's what poor Clint suffered from.

That's when it struck her that she'd be absolutely devastated if he did die. She still hardly knew the man, and yet the thought of him being dead tore at her heart. She blinked back tears of distress, not really sure what to do to help him, not sure whether there was a decent doctor in Skagway... realizing that if Clint died, she would have failed to help him find God again before his death. He would die so terribly lonely, and an unsaved man!

Chapter Fourteen

Then they cry unto the Lord in their trouble, and
He saveth them out of their distresses.
—Psalms 107:19

Elizabeth managed to dress quickly behind a shelf of supplies so Clint could not see her, although he seemed in no shape even to be aware of what was happening around him. She'd managed to wake the Wheelers in their upstairs apartment. Mrs. Wheeler loaned her some tea and a strainer, and Mr. Wheeler promised to find a doctor. However, it was now dawn, and still no doctor had arrived.

She finished buttoning her dress, leaving off most of her slips. Quickly she pulled her hair back and twisted it into a bun, shoving hairpins into it. On stockinged feet she searched for her shoes. Before she could find them, someone knocked at the back door. She walked closer. "Who is it?"

"It's Michael Wheeler. I found a doctor," came the reply.

Elizabeth unbolted the door and Wheeler walked in with another man who appeared to be in his fifties, with thinning hair that needed cutting, a scraggly gray beard and a mustache badly in need of a trim. He'd pulled on a woolen jacket and pants, but he wore no shirt. Rather, the top half of his long johns showed under his jacket. Elizabeth was relieved to see that he'd apparently realized the seriousness of Clint's situation and had hurriedly dressed, however, he certainly did not fit her idea of an educated physician.

"Doc Williams," the man mumbled as he hurried over to kneel beside the cot, where Clint still lay curled up.

"He coughed so hard that he threw up blood," Elizabeth told the man. She suspected Clint was not even aware of it. "I'm afraid I soiled one of your towels cleaning things up," she explained to Wheeler. "I'm so sorry."

"Don't worry about it," the man replied.

Again Elizabeth silently thanked God that she'd found at least one person with a bit of compassion in this wild town.

"I tried to get him to drink some tea," she told the doctor, "but he's so far gone I couldn't even get him awake enough to take any. He's burning up, Doctor Williams, and when he threw up blood like that—"

The doctor waved her off, pulling back the covers and forcing Clint onto his back. Clint flopped over as though half dead. Doctor Williams ripped open his shirt and the top half of his long johns without even stopping to unbutton anything first, then placed a stethoscope to Clint's chest. He moved it to his ribs, then managed to roll him forward so he could move the stethoscope to Clint's back. After a moment he pulled the stethoscope from his ears and took

Clint's pulse. Then he sighed and rose, facing Elizabeth and Wheeler.

"It's pneumonia, all right."

Elizabeth gasped with dread. "What can we do?"

Williams shook his head. "Not much, really. I've got some horse liniment you can heat up and rub on his chest, and if you keep a cool towel on his head—"

"*Horse* liniment?" Elizabeth interrupted.

"Yes, ma'am. Generally what works for a horse with pneumonia will work for a man with pneumonia, if it's God's will that he lives."

Elizabeth looked at Wheeler with a frown. Wheeler rubbed at the back of his neck. "He, uh, he's a horse doctor. Best thing I could find under the circumstances. Most doctors who come through here are on their way to Dawson. A real doctor is supposed to be on his way here to stay, but he hasn't made it yet."

Elizabeth looked back at the doctor, confused as to whether she should be grateful or angry. "A *horse* doctor?" she repeated.

"Ma'am, I've took care of humans lots of times. I've pulled teeth and delivered babies and even took out bullets a time or two. A horse has a heart and lungs and organs and blood and guts same as a man. Like I said, what works for pneumonia on a critter can sometimes work for a man, too." He reached inside his black bag and took out a fair-sized brown bottle. "This here stuff smells mostly like lemon, but it has a stink to it, too. Fact is, it's just possible the smell alone will rouse him and make him want to get better just so he can wash the stuff off. I guarantee it'll sink through and break up all that congestion inside of him so he can get rid of it, but he'll do a lot more coughin' first. This stuff will help bring down the fever, too. That's the most important thing."

Elizabeth was still trying to deal with the fact that a horse doctor was treating a man who was close to death.

"You take this here liniment and warm the bottle in hot water, then rub it all over his chest and a little on his back if you can manage to do that. Then keep him covered good and keep cold wet towels on his forehead to help bring down the fever. If God's of a mind to let him live, then he should be feelin' a lot better within about twenty-four hours."

Elizabeth blinked. Rub the liniment on his bare chest? "I...I wouldn't feel right touching his chest. Can't you do it?"

Williams frowned. "Well, he's your husband, ain't he?"

Elizabeth hesitated. She didn't want to lie, but she also realized how bad it might look if she didn't. She glanced at Wheeler. "Mr. Wheeler, I met this man on the ship coming here. He's just a friend because he helped me out a couple of times. I only brought him in here because I could see how sick he was and I felt responsible. I fell off the ship and he dived in after me. I fear his condition is worse because of going into that cold water to help me. I found him out in the lobby and gave him my cot to get him off the drafty floor. I can't...I mean, I shouldn't stay in here alone nursing him. How would it look? Isn't there someone who could help?"

Wheeler looked at Williams, who shook his head. "You're lucky I came over here at all," the doctor told her. "I'm leavin' in an hour or so for Dawson myself, so don't count on me." He walked up to Elizabeth and handed her the liniment. "Lady, if the man saved you from drownin', then the least you can do is rub some liniment on his chest and do whatever else you need to do to help him live." He headed for the back door. "Oh, and keep him a bit elevated," he added, "else his lungs could fill up and drown him."

"But—"

Williams turned to face her with a look that told her he'd done all he could do.

"How much do I owe you?" she asked.

"Nothin'."

The man turned and left, and Elizabeth faced Mr. Wheeler with questioning eyes.

Wheeler sighed and glanced at Clint, then back to Elizabeth. "Ma'am, most folks in this town are either coming back from somewhere or going somewhere or running businesses. I wouldn't know who to tell you to go to for help, and I kind of hate to have my wife help on account of she tends to take chest colds easy anyway and at her age—"

"I understand," Elizabeth told him. "I guess I'll just…do what I have to do."

Clint fell into another round of pitiful coughing and groaning, and Wheeler looked anxious to leave. "I'd help you myself, but if I get too close I could maybe somehow take something home to the wife, you know?"

Elizabeth closed her eyes, hiding her exasperation. "I understand. Thank you so much for going out in the dark and trying to find a doctor. That was very kind of you. I hope you don't mind letting me…us…use the room for however long it takes for Mr. Brady to feel better."

"That's fine. I won't even charge you."

"I deeply appreciate that, Mr. Wheeler."

The man patted her arm and left. Elizabeth bolted both doors and stood there a moment, clinging to the bottle of horse liniment, and in resignation leaning her forehead against the door, eyes closed in prayer.

"Lord, for some reason You have placed this burden on me. And so I accept it. And if I am the one who has to... touch Mr. Brady's bare chest, please understand that it's necessary to save his life and not a sinful act. Please work through my hands to heal this man who has done so much for me."

Steeling her resolve, she turned to face Clint, who lay hanging over the side of the cot coughing up more blood. It seemed incredible to think a man could drown lying in bed!

"Heaven help me," she whispered. She walked over to take the lid from the kettle of water on top of the potbelly stove, then loosened the cork on the horse liniment and set it into the water to warm it up.

While waiting for the horse liniment to warm, Elizabeth took a towel from a stack of several on a shelf and hung it over the elbow of the stove pipe to warm. She knelt beside Clint. His face was flushed with fever, and his rattled breathing was interspersed with groans. He appeared barely cognizant of her presence. God had given her a job to do, and do it she must.

She took a deep breath and grasped hold of one of Clint's hands, closing her eyes.

"Heavenly Father," she prayed, *"help me to look upon this man as Your child and not a stranger. Use my hands*

to help heal, and help me say the right words to him when he recovers. Guide me in every way, Lord Jesus, and please let Clint Brady live. More than that, I pray that somehow he finds his way back to You and can stop living the life he lives now. Thank You, Jesus. Amen."

With that, she rose and leaned closer, touching Clint's shoulder. "Clint, try to roll onto your back so I can put some liniment on you."

He did not respond.

"Clint? I need your help here." She pushed at his shoulder, and he groaned. "Clint, roll onto your back."

"Jenny?" he moaned.

Who was Jenny? His dead wife? Did he think she was Jenny? "Yes," she answered. "Roll over, Clint."

Finally he moved to lie flat on his back. Taking a deep breath for courage, Elizabeth pulled open his shirt, which had only two buttons left on it because of the way Dr. Williams had jerked it open. She turned and took the liniment from the kettle and poured some into the palm of her right hand, her eyebrows arching in reaction to the strong scent. If not for the mild scent of lemon, the concoction would literally stink, and she wondered that the strong aroma did not stir Clint fully awake.

She smeared the oily substance onto Clint's chest. She worked it along his ribs and around under him as far as she could get with him still on his back. By then she'd used up the first dose and poured more into her palm to smear over his upper chest, all the way to his neck. Hard as she tried to ignore it, she could not help thinking what a big, strong, brave man he was, or noticing how hard-muscled he was.

Nor could she avoid the odd curiosity touching his bare skin aroused in her thoughts.

She suddenly drew away, ashamed for wondering. *"God, forgive me,"* she whispered, turning to take the warmed towel from the stove pipe. She laid it over Clint's chest and pulled his shirt closed as best she could, then covered him. She washed her hands of the liniment and then poured fresh water into a bowl and wet a washrag with it. As she washed Clint's face with the cool rag, she realized he was already growing quite a stubble of a beard. Should she try to shave him? Surely he had a razor in his gear, but she'd never shaved anything in her life, and she feared cutting him. With any luck he would be well enough to shave himself in a day or two.

She rinsed the rag and wrung it out again, folding it and laying it across his forehead. Then she took hold of his hand again. "You're going to be all right, Clint," she said softly. "I'll not leave you until you're completely well."

To her surprise, he squeezed her hand. "Jenny?" he said again. "I'm so…sorry."

Elizabeth frowned, a thousand questions running through her mind. "For what?" she asked daringly, hoping to learn something more about this man's past.

"Couldn't…help," he muttered.

To Elizabeth's amazement, a tear slipped out of Clint's right eye and trickled down toward his ear. Pain tore through her heart at the sight. "It's all right," she answered, not sure if it might help. "I'm happy now. I'm safe and well."

"Take care of little Ethan," he whispered.

Ethan? There was someone else? A child? Did Clint

Brady have a son? If only she knew all the facts, she would know better the right things to say to this man. "I will," she answered. What else could she say to such a statement?

The moment was interrupted by another round of pitiful coughing and spitting. Clint groaned, and Elizabeth adjusted the pillows under him to make sure he remained slightly elevated. She gasped when Clint suddenly clamped his arms around her and pulled her tight against him, breathing the word *Jenny* into her ear.

"Don't go," he mumbled. "Stay…home."

Elizabeth was both stunned and touched. His grip was surprisingly strong, forcing her to move the rest of her body onto the side of the bed and lie bent over him, her head on his shoulder. The poor man actually thought she was his wife. If that thought might help him get better, she supposed she should stay in this position until he fell into a deeper sleep and let go of her again. He could, after all, be dying. Why not let him die thinking he was holding his wife?

Chapter Fifteen

A soft answer turneth away wrath:
but grievous words stir up anger.
—Proverbs 15:1

Clint awoke to an odd smell, what seemed a mixture of lemon and alcohol and God knew what else. It created a vapor that actually made it easier to breathe, although he remembered feeling so rotten that any kind of breathing would seem a relief.

He stirred, surprised to realize that he was not lying on a hard floor at all, but rather on something soft. He stretched and took a deep breath, realizing immediately that doing so was a bad idea. He coughed until it felt as though his very innards would come up through his throat, then noticed a bowl sitting on the floor by the bed. Having no other way to get rid of the phlegm that nearly choked him, he spat it into the bowl, then felt so weary he collapsed back onto the pillow with a groan.

"Clint?"

A woman spoke his name. He heard a rustling sound, and someone knelt beside him then, touching his face.

"Well, at least it seems your fever is gone," she said. "How do you feel? You haven't sneezed for quite some time, and it sounded like you were breathing just fine through your nose. Everything must have settled in your chest."

Clint squinted at her and saw by the dim light of an oil lamp that it was none other than Elizabeth Breckenridge. "Elizabeth?"

She smiled. "Yes. And it's so good to see that you seem to be getting a little better."

He raised up on an elbow again and looked around. "Where am I?"

She stood up. "You are in the storeroom of the hotel. Actually it's my room—the only room the manager had when I checked in two days ago."

He ran a hand through his hair, then felt the stubble on his face. "How long have I been in here?"

"For two days." Elizabeth pulled a wooden chair close to the bed and then told Clint about how she'd found him and the horse doctor who'd treated him.

Clint lay back down, staring at the low, sloped ceiling of the back room, trying to straighten his thoughts. "Two days?"

"Two days. For a while there I truly feared you would die. I've been praying constantly for you."

He coughed again, but not as deeply this time. *Two days*. His chest ached fiercely. He felt under the blanket and discovered he was still dressed. "What about…you mean

I haven't…" Lord, his bladder was full! "Is the manager out there?"

"I'm not sure. What's wrong?"

"What's *wrong?*" He rolled his eyes. Of all people to be left in charge of taking care of him, it had to be Elizabeth Breckenridge. Why not some whore from down the street? He felt humiliated at being sick and weak in front of her, embarrassed to tell her he needed the chamber pot or a privy, ashamed at how he must look, let alone how he must smell by now. "I haven't emptied my bladder for two days, *that's* what's wrong!" he answered, angry that he should even have to explain.

"Oh!" Elizabeth jumped up from her chair and practically ran out the door, returning a few long minutes later with a nearly bald man sporting a red beard and wearing the typical denim pants and calico shirt of most men in the area.

"There he is," Elizabeth told the man, before quickly shutting the door.

"Name's Victor Macklevoy," the man told him. "The lady grabbed my arm out in the lobby and told me you need to get to the privy out back. She told me to come help you out so's you don't fall down on the way." He chuckled and held out his arm. "Let's go."

Furious with humiliation, Clint refused the man's arm. "I can do this alone, thank you. All she had to do was tell me where the blasted outhouse is!" He wrapped a blanket around his shoulders and reached for his boots, grumbling profanities as he yanked them on. "Appreciate the help, mister, but you can go on about your business."

Fighting dizziness and determined not to lean on

someone else, he managed to get himself outside to take care of things. Going back inside, he vowed to wash and change and get out of Elizabeth's room.

"Of all people to be taking care of me," he muttered. Pain seared through his chest again, and by the time he reached the bed he realized with great frustration that indeed he was too weak even to wash himself, let alone change his clothes and leave. It felt as if a volcano was erupting inside him, and his muscles felt like mush. He'd never been sick a day in his life! How did this happen, and why now?

He knew why. Because he was so involved in feelings for Miss High-and-Mighty-Perfect Breckenridge that he'd dived into that cold water to save her. If he'd had any sense at all he would have let her drown! He'd thought he was rid of her, and now here he was lying in her bed and totally dependent on her to take care of him until he could find enough strength to get out of here.

Someone knocked on the door. "Clint?"

"Heaven help me," he groaned quietly. "It's okay," he said louder.

Elizabeth came inside, great concern in her pretty green eyes. "You must still be so weak."

"I'm all right," he grumped. He curled back into the blankets. "Tell the manager that as soon as a room is free, he's to give it to you. I can get by okay on my own now."

"You most certainly cannot! I will go out and see about bringing back something for you to eat. You'll need food to get your strength back, and lots more rest."

"Aren't you supposed to be headed for Dawson?"

She sat down in the nearby chair again. "Yes. But after

everything you've done for me, do you really think I could have left you, as sick as you were?"

He closed his eyes in exasperation. "Why not? You could have got me that doctor and then left two days ago."

"With you coughing so badly that I thought you'd choke to death? Let alone the fact that you were so hot I half expected you to burst into flames! You were, and still are, I might remind you, a very sick man. I kept that liniment warm and kept putting it on you. It truly does seem to have helped."

He thought a moment. *Elizabeth* had put the liniment on his bare chest? Just a few days ago she was mortified that he'd dared even to take off his shirt in front of her. Their gazes met, and she seemed to have read his thoughts. She quickly looked away, getting up from the chair and pretending to fuss with some towels.

"What do you feel like eating?" she asked. "There is a little diner just across the street and a short way down. I tried to get you to eat, but it's been impossible to do anything more than get some water down your throat. You must be famished." She went to a coat stand and took down a cape, putting it around her shoulders, then finally faced him again.

He turned on his back and stared at the ceiling again. "I wish you would just get a room for yourself and leave me alone."

"You know that I can't do that. I have a responsibility—"

"Will you quit with all that? We're even-up now. Thanks for getting me some help. And, yes, if you want, you can get me something that will stick to my ribs, something like biscuits and gravy, I guess. And I could stand a couple of shots of whiskey."

The room hung silent for a moment. "Very well. I'll get you the biscuits and gravy…and some hot tea," she answered. She went out the back door.

"Hot tea," Clint mimicked. He thought about it a moment. The prim and proper Miss Breckenridge had probably never tasted whiskey or even touched a bottle of it. He rolled his eyes at the thought of drinking *tea* after coming out of the worst sickness a man could suffer!

He sat up again, then wrapped himself in one of the blankets and stood up. This was a storeroom. It was a good bet there was some whiskey around here somewhere. He searched through several of the shelves, struggling not to fall down he was so weak and dizzy. Being careful not to disturb the manager's neat stacking of supplies, he finally caught sight of a couple of brown bottles. He pulled one out from the shelf and uncorked it, taking a sniff.

He grinned. "Now *here's* what I need!" he said. With that he took a long swallow. "Best medicine in the world for what ails a man."

Chapter Sixteen

*They mount up to the heavens, they go down again
to the depths: their soul is melted because of
trouble. They reel to and fro, and stagger like a
drunken man, and are at their wit's end.*
—Psalms 107:26 & 27

Elizabeth lifted her skirts slightly as she hurriedly made her way across the street on wooden planks that had been put down to create pathways at frequent intervals all along the muddy thoroughfare of Skagway. Getting across safely was yet another feat. There was a constant flow of traffic, people, horses, wagons, dogs and sleds.

"Looks like it's blowin' up a good one in the passes," she heard a man comment. She glanced at him, then looked in the direction he was looking. Snow was visible in the higher mountains, which reminded her that it was becoming dangerously late for making it to Dawson.

Once she got some food for Clint, she really needed to

get out today and find someone with whom she could travel safely…and leave soon. Clint was too sick for it, and he'd already made it clear that he did not intend to take her any farther himself. Besides, now he was too sick to leave any time soon.

She made her way past men of such diverse looks and clothing that she wondered if there might be a sampling of every human male on earth right here in Skagway. Some wore neat suits and top hats and were clean-shaven; others sported the bristle of a few days without a shave while yet more sported full-grown beards and mustaches. Many wore soiled, tattered clothing; while most wore the common clothing of the everyday prospector: dark woolen pants, plaid shirts, vests and jackets, woolen caps with ear flaps, most wearing leather boots, some wearing shoes with steel cleats, and some wearing simple canvas shoes. Most were courteous, a few made unmentionable remarks that she ignored, and nearly all eyed her curiously.

She entered the restaurant, where tables full of men stared as she walked through to the back to ask a very tired-looking waitress for some food to take to "a sick friend."

The waitress, whom Elizabeth had never seen before in the establishment, looked her over disdainfully. "Lady, can't you see how busy I am serving the customers out there? You want special service? Go talk to the owner." She nodded toward a gray-haired man who was giving orders to a cook.

Determined not to be intimidated by the rude waitress, Elizabeth walked up to the owner with the same request.

"It'll cost you a dollar," the man grumped.

"A dollar! That's outrageous!"

The man grinned through yellow teeth. "Honey, it ain't outrageous in Skagway! You think I was dumb enough to come here for *gold?*" He leaned closer, his breath atrocious. "I'm makin' *my* money off all the *rest* that's come here for gold! A man's got to eat, don't he?" He chuckled and straightened. "Besides, yer askin' for somethin' extra. Now, do you want what you asked for, or not?"

Elizabeth reminded herself that even this repulsive man who was literally stealing from everyone in his restaurant was a child of God. "Fine," she answered, digging into her skirt pocket. She handed him two fifty-cent pieces. "Please hurry. My friend has been very sick and hasn't eaten in two or three days."

The man shrugged and shouted an order to another cook. Both cooks were women who looked quite harried and overworked. The owner looked at Elizabeth again. "You make sure I get back my dishes and the tray," he told her. "I'll come lookin' for ya' if ya' don't." He grinned. "You wouldn't be holed up at some whorehouse, would you?"

Elizabeth stiffened. "I'm at Wheeler's Hotel," she answered curtly. "And you needn't worry. You'll get your tray back, although for a whole dollar, I should get to keep it!"

Regretting her sharp tongue, she stood back and waited, noticing filth on the floor and hoping that after being so sick, Clint would not end up dying from eating the food she brought back to him. Minutes later one of the cooks arranged the food on a plate and set it on a tray, covering it with a towel. She then poured coffee into a pewter pot and set the pot and a tin cup on the tray. "Here you go, ma'am," the woman told her.

"Thank you, and God bless you," Elizabeth answered, feeling sorry for the overworked woman. The cook just stared at her a moment, obviously surprised at her last remark. She smiled. "Why, thank you," she told Elizabeth. "That's a nice thing to say."

Elizabeth took the tray, smiling in return, and feeling better that she'd said something kind rather than let the owner make her rude to everyone else. She left, thinking how people and places like this were such a test of one's faith and one's desire to be kind to others.

She made her way to the hotel and after briefly relating Clint's condition to Mr. Wheeler she entered the storeroom.

"Here you are!" she told Clint as she set the tray on the only table in the room. "I have eggs and ham and biscuits and coffee! It cost me a whole dollar, but you need to start eating." She turned to face him. "I think you'll—" She did not finish her sentence. There sat Clint Brady, with a look on his face she couldn't even read, a brown bottle in his hand. He held it up.

"How about a toast, Miss Christian-Holier-than-Thou Breckenridge? What does your Bible say about a woman drinking whiskey? Jesus drank wine, I think, didn't He?" He chuckled. "Maybe He wasn't so perfect after all." He waved her over. "Come on. Take a swig. This stuff will cure anything that ails you. I drink enough of this and I'll be back to my old self within twenty-four hours."

Elizabeth's heart fell. "I just spent a whole dollar on you, Clint Brady, and I come back to find you *drunk!*"

He winked at her. "Don't worry. I'll eat the food, soon as I finish this bottle."

Elizabeth felt like crying. "You can finish it alone, Mr. Brady, and if you do, I highly doubt you will be one-hundred-percent cured by tomorrow. It is more likely you'll hardly be able to get out of bed!"

He laughed again. "You have an answer for everything, don't you? What the heck does it take to get you to loosen up, Miss God's-Gift-to-the-World?"

"Certainly not whiskey! And no, I *don't* have the answer for everything. I don't have an answer for why you behave the way you do." She folded her arms, struggling to control her fury and deciding to say something that would wipe the drunken smile off his face. "One thing I don't know is— who is Jenny? You called me Jenny a couple of times while you were your sickest. Was she your wife, Clint? What happened to her?"

The remark certainly *did* wipe the smile off his face— to a greater extent than she'd thought it would. The smile turned to a grim look, his blue eyes suddenly looking much darker. "Get out!" he told her. "Get out of here before I knock you clear out the back door!"

He rose, making ready to come for her, and Elizabeth backed away. The anger in his eyes was unnerving. She grasped the door handle, but before Clint could reach her he wavered, then fell flat on his face.

Chapter Seventeen

An ungodly man diggeth up evil: and in his lips
there is as a burning fire.

—Proverbs 16:27

Clint awoke to a raging headache. Unaware at first of where he was, he rolled onto his back and rubbed his forehead, finding there a swollen knot. He squinted with pain, taking a moment to think. The room was dark except for an oil lamp burning low.

Skagway. He was in Skagway…and he'd been so sick he'd wanted to die. The darkness could mean practically any time of day, since daylight hours were getting shorter and shorter this time of year. Was it morning or evening? With a groan he sat up, running his hands through his hair, which he realized was getting long. He scratched at his face and frowned at the long stubble there.

He took a deep breath, thinking more, looking around the room. He spotted a brown bottle nearby. That was when it hit him. Whiskey! He'd drunk practically that whole bottle of whiskey! It wasn't a big bottle, but big enough. No wonder he felt so lousy. And he remembered something about food…Elizabeth…she'd brought him food…said something about paying a whole dollar for it.

He managed to get to his knees, then realized he'd been lying on the floor. He stood up and stumbled back to the bed. He sat down on it and looked at the floor, groaning. Had he passed out in front of Elizabeth Breckenridge?

He shook his head and ran his hands through his hair yet again. It all came back to him, and he moaned. What had he done? After all Elizabeth had done for him, and he'd threatened to clobber her! What kind of man had he become?

He walked over to the little table where the oil lamp sat, and he turned it up so he could see the room better. On the stove sat a tin plate with food on it, and a pewter coffeepot. He walked closer to see that the tray held eggs and ham, although quite dried out now. Elizabeth must have put the food there to keep it warm for him…and after he'd as much as cussed her out and chased her out of here. He checked the coffeepot and found it full, and still hot from sitting on the little potbelly stove, which she must have stoked with wood before leaving.

He glanced at the bed and saw that the sheets had been changed. Everything was clean and neat…kind of like Jenny used to take care of things. Clean clothes were laid out for him. For God's sake, had she gone and had his clothes washed?

A further glance around the room showed that all of Elizabeth's things were gone. Hadn't he told her to get a room of her own? She must have done so, which would probably cost her more than this back room had. Or maybe she'd found someone to take her on to Dawson.

No! He couldn't let her do that! There wasn't a man in this town who could be trusted to take her alone on a long trip like that. But then, maybe he couldn't even trust himself under the same circumstances. Apparently not, judging by his most recent behavior.

Never had he felt like such a complete ass. His aching head made him want to lie back down for several more hours, but he had to do something about this mess. He needed to apologize to Elizabeth. He needed to find out if she'd already left for Dawson. If so, he had to go after her and order her to go with no one but him.

He felt as if someone had beat him near to death and dragged him behind a horse for a few miles, but he was better and could do the rest of his healing on the journey. There was no time to be wasted! What was the date? How late was too late to head for Dawson? Were the horses he'd boarded still all right? For all he knew they'd been sold out from under him, or stolen.

The last few days were like a nightmare of sickness and dizziness and being hardly aware of where he was or what was going on around him. Then he'd had to go and drink that whiskey, thinking it would cure what was left of his pneumonia. Thing was, he'd drank it for another reason, like he always did—to forget. Forget. Forget. Whiskey eased the pain in his heart, but then sometimes it only made things worse, so he'd drink till he passed out. When a man was that far gone, he couldn't think about anything at all.

Now he did have to think! He was a mess, needed a shave, needed to change, needed to go find Elizabeth, needed to apologize, needed to get a map showing the best route to Dawson, needed to get the proper supplies, needed to go claim his horses...and he'd practically forgotten about Roland Fisher! The man was worth five thousand dollars!

This sickness had put him behind on everything and had shown him up to be a weak man in front of Elizabeth. He'd sure never let that happen again! What must she think of him!

Quickly he turned and scarfed down the dried, rubbery eggs and ham and toast, washing all of that down with the coffee that had become strong from sitting so long. There, that felt better. He took a porcelain bowl from a shelf, along with a towel and some bar soap and poured water from a kettle into the bowl.

He undressed and began vigorously washing himself, then rummaged through his things to find his shaving mug, brush and razor. A mirror hung on the wall near the door, so he moved the small table there so he could shave, wincing when he nicked his jaw. He washed his face again, then put on the clothes Elizabeth left out for him. He picked up his comb and walked back to the mirror, combing back his disheveled hair as best he could, thinking how he'd better get it cut before he left for Dawson. Then again, why bother? On a trip like that a man might as well not worry about shaving or cutting his hair until he arrived at his destination.

He walked to the back door to check the temperature outside. Cool and rainy. Could he have expected anything else? Seemed more like late evening than morning. He scurried to the privy to take care of personals, then went back inside and took his fur-lined suede jacket from a hook. Under the jacket hung his gun belt and six-gun. Deciding not to wear those just now, he pulled on his jacket, then drank down more coffee to help sober himself more before going through the door that led to the hotel lobby. The manager was at his desk.

"Wheeler, isn't it?" he spoke up, walking up to the man.

"Well, Mr. Brady! You're looking quite a bit better! Glad to see you up and around! Did you enjoy the food Miss Breckenridge brought you yesterday?"

"Yesterday?" Elizabeth must not have said anything to the man about his being drunk. "Yes. It really hit the spot," he answered. "Can you tell me what time it is? And where is Miss Breckenridge now? Her things are gone."

"Yes! I finally had a decent room open up." He winked. "I think she was happy to get a room of her own. She seems like such a nice young lady."

Clint's feelings of guilt kept getting worse. "Yes, she is. Which room is hers?"

"Well, it's upstairs—first door on the right, but she's not there. She went to get something to eat, and then she wanted to try to find someone who might accompany her to Dawson. I told her about a town meeting just up the street where men are gathered to learn more about the trip. But I also tried to tell her there are few men in this town she could trust. She insisted—"

Clint did not wait to hear the rest of the man's sentence. He hurried out the door to find Elizabeth.

Chapter Eighteen

*The simple believeth every word: but the prudent
man looketh well to his going.*

—Proverbs 14:15

"Well, lady, first you have to take either Chilkoot Pass
or White Pass to get to Lake Bennett. If you're real lucky,
you'll still have all your provisions with you. Now, if ya
can't get all yer supplies over there yerself, then you'll pay
about triple what it costs to buy them here, if'n you have
to buy them from those that carry them over for you, so yer
best off gettin' them to Lake Bennett yerself, ya know
what I mean?"

Elizabeth just stared at the bearded, kind-eyed older
man who called himself only by the nickname of Hard
Tack. He was obviously enjoying being able to show her
how much he knew about the trip to the Yukon. He'd rattled
on so fast that she was left totally confused.

"Now, I'd shore like to take ya myself," he continued,

"only I ain't goin' all the way, on account of I take supplies just to Lake Bennett. I kin git ya that far, if that helps, but then ya'd have to find somebody else to help you git the rest of the way, which is by boat up the Yukon River, over dangerous rapids and all that." He looked her over. "Ma'am, I'd suggest ya wait till spring myself."

"I'd really rather go now," she answered. "I don't know what on earth I would do with myself in a place like Skagway all winter. Besides, I can't afford room and board for that long. I guess I could get a job, but all I want is to reach my brother in Dawson and have it over with. There I could rest at last and truly be home and with someone familiar."

The man scratched his beard. "Well, now, I know that that group of fellas over there is goin' for sure, leavin' in a couple of days. One of 'em is a lawyer, so he says. The others are just friends of his, all businessmen, they claim, 'cept in these parts ya can't always believe what a man tells ya. I reckon ya can trust them as good as anybody."

Elizabeth glanced at the group of men gathered in a large tent with about one hundred others who'd come to hear about what they would need for their trip to the Klondike. Those here to fill them in were outfitters and owners of Skagway supply stores, as well as men with horses, dogs, sleds and boats for sale.

The men Hard Tack referred to were mostly dressed in suits and overcoats, certainly not men who appeared to know much about survival in the wilds. Still, as Hard Tack said, they certainly appeared to be gentlemen who would at least honor her integrity and would surely protect her if need be from animals and the elements. She thanked Hard

Tack and walked over to the men, who were intently listening to a man telling them about the proper way to pitch a tent on hard, cold, rocky ground, giving tips on what to do if the snow was deep. It was obvious by comments some of the men made that indeed, they didn't know much about such things. One of them turned to eye her, then removed his hat. "Ma'am?"

Elizabeth took a deep breath for courage, hating to approach strangers with her request. "My name is Elizabeth Breckenridge, and that man over there—" She pointed to Hard Tack. "He's a supplier, and he told me you and your friends might oblige my request."

The man smiled through thin lips and looked her over with rather unreadable brown eyes. He was neither handsome nor hard to look at, with dark hair that seemed too thin for what appeared to be a man only perhaps Clint's age, which she guessed to be late twenties or perhaps thirty. "And what might that request be?"

"Well, I'm headed for Dawson myself, to find my brother, Peter. He's a preacher there." She hoped that fact would cement her own credibility and honor. "I need some kind of escort on the trip, and I was hoping…well, Hard Tack…he said you were a lawyer here with some other businessmen. I hoped that meant you were all gentlemen and that perhaps I could trust you to get me to Dawson. I wouldn't be any burden, I promise. I could cook for all of you, keep your clothes washed and mended, that kind of thing. I can't really afford to pay—"

"Certainly!" the man answered before she could finish. His grin widened. "We'd be honored to take you along with us, Miss Breckenridge!" He touched the arm of one of his friends, a portly, middle-aged fellow wearing a suit. "Jonathan Hedley, meet Miss Elizabeth Breckenridge."

Hedley nodded to her as the first man put out his hand.

"And my name is Ezra Faine, ma'am." He looked at Hedley. "Miss Breckenridge needs an escort to Dawson, wondered if we might be obliged to help her out."

Hedley's eyebrows shot up with pleasure as he grinned, his cheeks actually turning red. "Why, of course we would!" the man answered, too quickly it seemed to Elizabeth. He turned to Ezra and winked.

"We leave in two days, Miss Breckenridge," Ezra told her. "We and our friends would be glad to take you along with us. We'll make sure you get to Dawson all safe and sound. Do you have all the supplies you need?"

Someone in the crowded tent bumped Elizabeth's velvet hat, and she adjusted it as she answered. "Actually no. I mean, I just don't have the money—"

"Not to worry," Ezra told her. "We have brought along plenty of money, and we'll get all the necessary supplies. You just bring along your personal baggage and we'll make room." He leaned closer, grinning eagerly. "You, uh, don't have any other female friends you could bring along, do you?"

Elizabeth frowned. "What?"

The man put an arm around her shoulders and led her aside. "Ma'am, we both know that it's pretty unlikely a woman traveling alone to Dawson is totally proper, if you know what I mean. Now, I'll accept your story about having a brother there who is a preacher. That's what we'll tell the others. But, well, it's possible we could get caught in a blizzard or something like that, which means we'd have to all hole up in a tent together. Now I know that even a woman who's, uh, not so proper, shall we say?—that even she wouldn't want to put up with a whole tent full of men. Me, I'll have my own tent, and I'll see you get to Dawson without charging you one blessed cent, as long as you share my tent with me, if you know what I mean."

Elizabeth's heart fell like a rock. This man thought she was lying about Peter! He thought she was a prostitute trying to hook a free ride to Dawson! Fury and disappointment engulfed her, and she could not hide her tears as she looked at Ezra Faine. "You are a filthy-minded, reprehensible man with not one ounce of manners or honor about you!" she shot back.

The man grasped her arm. "Now, honey, don't get angry. I just wanted to be sure—"

"Let go of the lady," came a deep voice.

Elizabeth recognized it as Clint's. Ezra glanced up at someone tall standing behind her. "What was that?" he asked.

"You heard me. Take your hand off her arm. And if I were you, I'd turn around and rejoin my friends and not say one more word."

Ezra gave Elizabeth a light shove before he let go of her. "Says who?" he asked, trying to look brave and manly.

"Mister, I'm a bounty hunter, so hurting or killing a man means nothing to me. Is that enough of an answer?"

Ezra backed away slightly, looking Clint over and pretending not to be afraid. He moved his gaze to Elizabeth. "He one of your customers or something?"

In the next split second a big fist came from behind Elizabeth and slammed into Ezra Faine's face, sending the man sprawling into a stack of sacks stuffed with beans. One of them broke, spilling the contents onto the wooden floor. Beans bounced about, some of them off Ezra's face. Other men turned to look, and Clint grasped Elizabeth's arm. "Let's go," he told her.

Still fighting tears, Elizabeth left with him.

Chapter Nineteen

For we must all appear before the judgment seat of
Christ; that everyone may receive the things done
in His body, according to that He hath done,
whether it be good or bad.
                                    —1 Corinthians 5:10

Clint walked so fast that he nearly dragged Elizabeth
along the boardwalk back toward the hotel.

"Clint Brady, how dare you!"

"How dare I what? Keep you from making the biggest
mistake of your life?"

"And you haven't made any?"

"I've made *plenty!*" He scooped her up in his arms to
carry her across one of the narrow board crosswalks.

"What are you doing!"

"Keeping you out of the mud."

"Not long ago you wanted to knock me clear out the
back door, if I remember your words correctly!"

"Yeah, well, that's what I want to talk about."

Elizabeth could not help being surprised at how adeptly he picked her up, as though she weighed nothing. He couldn't possibly be anywhere near his normal strength, but he'd clobbered Ezra Faine with startling force.

They reached the boardwalk at the other side of the street, and Elizabeth felt a sudden, surprising surge of happiness and desire rush through her as she looked at Clint Brady by the soft light of the oil lamps hanging along the boardwalk. It so startled her that she fought it vehemently.

"Put me down!" she commanded, tears coming again and making her even more embarrassed and upset with herself.

Clint just stood there with her for a moment, an odd look in his eyes, almost like a sorry little boy—a look that changed to something she could not quite decipher. Sorrow? Adoration? For one brief moment she thought he might actually kiss her!

"Tell me you aren't afraid of me. I'm sorry for what I said, and we need to talk."

"We certainly do! And you owe me a dollar for that wasted food!"

Clint set her on her feet. "It wasn't wasted. I ate all of it." He put a hand to her back. "Come on back to the hotel with me." He started walking again, a little slower this time.

"Why did you hit that poor man?"

"Poor man? Why were you crying?"

Elizabeth wiped at the tears on her cheeks. "I don't know."

"I think it was because the man was insulting you in some way, maybe misunderstood your intentions. Am I right?"

"Yes," she answered, embarrassed.

"You'd go a long way to find a man out of that crowd who'd honestly see you got to Dawson safely. Most would probably have every good intention of helping you out, but men are men, and each one at that tent is out for himself. You get snowed in with any one of them, worse than that, a group of them, and all their good intentions could easily go right out the smokehole and blow away with the mountain winds."

"And I suppose you're different?"

They were nearly at the hotel. "Maybe not, except for one thing."

"Oh? And what is that?"

They walked up the steps to the hotel front door, where he turned to face her before going in. "I care about you."

The comment left Elizabeth speechless for the moment. *I care about you.* What the heck did that mean? As just a friend? As something *more* than a friend? Heavens! What if *that* was what he meant?

The thought made her suddenly self-conscious. What was she supposed to say to him? Should she ask him what he meant? Did she *want* him to care about her as more than a friend? Truth was, deep inside, she did. She'd never really allowed the thought to surface until now. Still, he was nowhere near the kind of man she'd always imagined she'd end up with someday, and he was too old, wasn't he? Heck, she had no idea *how* old he was. Perhaps his size and experience made him seem older than he really was. And for heaven's sake, he killed men for money! He didn't even believe in God any more…or at least so he claimed. She suspected that wasn't true at all. *Dear Lord, what am*

I supposed to say? What should I do? What does this man want? What do You *want?*

Clint led her inside. Elizabeth was glad to see that Mr. Wheeler was not at his desk as they stormed through the lobby and into the back room. Clint closed the door and turned up the lamp. He ordered Elizabeth to sit down in the wooden chair, and Clint sat down on the cot. He took a deep breath, resting his elbows on his knees. Elizabeth waited for him to speak first, still a little wary of him after his drunken threat to her the day before.

"Here's the deal," he told her. "I've rescued you from peril twice, and you just might have saved *my* life. For some reason we keep running into each other and helping each other out. And now I've come to know you too well just to let you go off to Dawson with complete strangers, and too well to…well, like I said, I care about you, which means I could never…you know…take advantage, if the issue were to arise."

Elizabeth felt the odd rush of desire again, a feeling that confused her. With it came an uncomfortable embarrassment at what he meant.

"What I mean is," he continued, "I've come to respect you highly. What happened earlier…I can promise you that won't happen again. I drank that whiskey because whiskey can be a pretty good cure-all for a lot of things. I figured it would make me feel better and heal faster. Fact is, I feel awful. My head feels like it's trying to lift away from my neck, and my chest still hurts, but I think that by day after tomorrow, I could start for Dawson."

"That's too soon."

He put up his hand. "I'm not finished." He coughed before continuing. "I want to apologize for what I said earlier. You can rest assured I've never hit a woman in my life and never would. That was whiskey talking."

"And what if you drink during our journey?"

He held her gaze for a moment, and she thought again how blue his eyes were, how handsome he was.

"Well, I promise not to. You'll just have to believe me. But if I *do* drink—and even if I don't—you have to promise me one thing. One thing, and I'll get you to Dawson safely."

She frowned. "What is that?"

"Don't bring up my dead wife's name again."

So, that was it. Why was it so terrible to talk about Jenny? "And what if *you* bring it up?"

He shrugged. "I won't. But if I *were* to bring it up, it would be because I want to talk about her and…what happened to her…and…our son."

A son! Elizabeth could see just the mere mention of both of them made him agitated. "All right," she told him. "But may I say one thing?"

He eyed her warily. "What?"

Elizabeth swallowed before continuing. "Well, I just want you to know—" *God, help me find the right words* "—that I care about you, too. And the couple of times I did mention your family, I was just hoping to help you cope with loss…because that's just the kind of person I am. My heart is filled with the love of Jesus Christ and with His teachings and commandments, which means He would want me to be His instrument of healing in any way I can. So I just want you to know that if and when you should ever want to talk, I am ready and willing to listen, and I would never, ever judge your anger or the things it has made you do. I look at you and I see someone who I believe was once a wonderful family man who believed in God and in His Son, Jesus Christ."

Clint just stared at her a moment, and she could see a hunger in his eyes, but it quickly vanished. "Now there's another requirement. I don't want to be preached to for the whole journey."

Elizabeth smiled softly. "All right. I'll do my best." She folded her arms. "We never even said flat-out that we would do this, you know—go to Dawson together, I mean. I take it that's the decision you've made, considering the way you walked over to that tent and hauled me out of there and warned me not to trust anyone but you. I'm still not so sure I *can* trust you. But I am going to for the simple reason that I absolutely cannot believe that God didn't bring you into my life for the specific purpose of seeing that I reach Peter safely. If you are the one He's chosen for the job, then I have no choice but to trust you."

Clint actually smiled a little himself then. He took off his coat. "Thanks for fixing things up for me, changing the sheets and all. I'll pay you back for that meal, and I'll pay for your room. You shouldn't have had to take a different one."

"I'll manage."

"Okay, rule number three. Don't argue with me about everything. Whatever I tell you to do, you'll do it, including letting me pay for things. I have plenty of money and nothing to spend it on. I have even more in a bank in San Francisco. And no, it didn't *all* come from killing men for bounty. And yes, I'll explain all of it to you in my own time. And I might add that you have some explaining of your own to do."

Elizabeth raised her eyebrows in curiosity. "Oh? What do you mean?"

"I mean it's kind of strange that a nice young woman like you is headed for Dawson all alone. You said your father had been a preacher in San Francisco, and so had your brother, apparently. You must have belonged to a church. There must have been friends and parishioners who cared about you. Why the sudden rush to head for Dawson so late in the year? It can't be just because your mother died. You act more like someone who is running away from something. What is it you aren't telling me?"

Elizabeth felt the renewed shame and anger she'd felt when the deacons accused her of sinfully throwing herself at Reverend Selby. Would this man understand? Or would he judge her in the way so many men in the church had judged her? "I guess I'll have to answer that the way you said you felt about talking about your wife. I'll tell you when the time is right."

Clint rose. "Fair enough." He walked to the door and opened it. "One more rule," he added.

Elizabeth stood up and faced him. "What is that?"

"While we're traveling together, we lead others to believe we're husband and wife. If and when we come across people who knew us here in Skagway, we tell them we got married."

Elizabeth felt a flutter in her stomach. "Why?"

"Because you'll be safer if others think you're married. I shouldn't have to explain the reason why."

"But…if we sleep in separate tents—"

"We won't. Between lonely men and wild animals, I'm not letting you away from my protection. Besides, two tents mean extra gear to carry. A lot of the time we'll sleep out in the open anyway."

"But…I…"

"You're supposed to trust me. Besides, God sent me to help you, remember? He must mean for you to trust me."

Elizabeth thought about what a big, strong man he was, a man who carried a gun at that. Still, he was right. She'd said herself that God meant for them to travel together. Maybe she'd stuck her foot in her mouth, but what was done was done, and if she wanted to reach Peter safely, she didn't have much choice. Clint Brady was her best bet.

She nodded. "All right. From here on we are husband and wife. And you should start calling me Liz. That's what everyone close to me calls me. It will make us more believable."

"Good enough." He stood aside. "Good night…Liz. Be ready tomorrow morning at eight o'clock to go shopping with me. We need supplies and you need a wedding band. I'll have to go get my horses from where they are boarded and we'll start packing what we'll need."

"Do you know the way?"

"I have good maps, and besides, the trail is pretty well worn by now. We're bound to run into others the whole way."

Elizabeth walked through the door and looked back at him. "Thank you, Clint."

He nodded. "You're welcome. Use the rest of today and tomorrow to rest up. I'll be doing the same."

He closed the door and Elizabeth stared at it for a moment before turning to go to her room. *"Lord, what in the world are You doing?"* she muttered. This was going to be one interesting trip. Not only was Clint Brady a bounty hunter and a Godless man who needed her help in finding his faith…but he'd become more. She'd never thought her trip to Dawson would include a battle with her own heart.

Chapter Twenty

...Oh, my Father, if it be possible, let this cup pass from me: nevertheless, not as I will, but as Thou wilt.

—St. Matthew 26:39

"I'm glad I already have my own tinware," Clint told Elizabeth, who was watching him yank leather straps and tie ropes and hoist more supplies onto his three sturdy horses. "You can't find a tin plate or cup at any supply store. They're bought out. One man told me that last year you could pick up practically everything you needed for free as you went over the pass, so many supplies were abandoned by men who just gave up."

They stood behind Morgan's Supply Store, loading all the things Clint had purchased for their journey. Elizabeth felt so indebted. He'd not asked her for a dime.

Clint took a moment to glance at the surrounding mountains, and Elizabeth knew he was worried. Every peak showed snow, and the owner of the store where they'd purchased most of their grub, extra blankets, a tent and numerous other necessities, had told them that men who worked for him making deliveries had returned just the day before, giving up an effort to get over the pass to take valuable supplies on to Dawson. A sudden snowstorm had forced them back to Skagway.

"Could very likely be sunny and melting now," the store owner had suggested. "That's how it is here, a storm one minute, springlike weather the next. And if it does warm up, watch out for a sudden flood. A little mountain waterfall can turn into a raging torrent in five minutes flat."

The news was not inviting.

"Clint, are you sure you're up to this? You're still coughing, and I can tell you've lost weight."

"I'm all right," he insisted as he continued packing flour, pork, beans, coffee, sugar, tea, lard, potatoes, a shovel, two bags of oats for the horses, the tent, blankets and two rifles.

"I should have taught you how to use a gun," he told her as he shoved the rifles into their sheaths. "Could come in handy if a grizzly decides to have us for lunch. Most should be going into hibernation any time, so we might not have a problem. Then, of course, there are cougars to worry about, and wolves. If we're lucky, I'll come across a rabbit or deer so we can save our provisions, and we can always throw out a net every night while we travel the Yukon and eat fish instead of using up the salt pork. I have a good filleting knife, and a good hunting knife for cleaning game." He stopped and faced her. "Have you ever cleaned a rabbit or helped gut a deer?"

The thought was not pleasing. "I'm afraid not."

Clint shook his head. "You'll learn soon enough." He
returned to his packing.

"I'll do whatever I have to do to help," Elizabeth told
him. "I have no qualms about doing anything that's necessary to survive, including—" She eyed his six-gun. *You
are traveling with someone who kills men as easily as
rabbits,* she reminded herself. Was she crazy? "—including learning to use a rifle," she finished. "For all we know,
I might need to know that to help you out of some kind
of danger."

He faced her again, this time smiling. "If I am in a fist-
fight with a bear, I'm not sure I want you pointing a rifle
anywhere in my direction," he told her. "If the bear doesn't
get me, a bullet probably would."

She was astonished at how a genuine smile transformed
him completely, into a handsome, affable-looking man
who could be anyone's neighbor. She could not help
smiling in return. "Wouldn't a bullet be more humane than
letting you be mauled and slowly eaten by a grizzly?"

This time he chuckled. "You have a point."

Elizabeth leaned against a post as he continued packing.
He'd given her specific instructions not to try to help. He
had a method to his packing, and he didn't want any arguments about it. *I've done nothing but travel and sleep out
under the stars for the last four years,* he'd told her.

Hunting men, she'd thought. If she had her way, Clint
Brady would be a changed man by the time they reached
Dawson. How she would accomplish that, she had no idea.
God would have to do it through her.

She looked down at the plain gold band on her left hand.

Secretly, she liked the looks of it, the thought of being a wife someday...someday. She shook away the thought.

Their journey would start tomorrow, early in the morning. She pressed a hand to her stomach, feeling butterflies. Her father must be turning over in his grave knowing she was venturing out alone with a man who in all essence was really still a stranger...a man who sometimes liked his demon whiskey. He'd packed two full bottles of it, *for medicinal purposes,* he'd told her. *Whiskey can clean wounds and help a cough and clear sinuses and kill pain. Any man would be crazy to set out on a trip like this without some good whiskey along.*

She walked around to pat his horses, wanting them to get to know her. One was a black gelding named Devil, who, Clint advised "fit his name." She'd already been instructed to leave Devil to him to handle. Still, the horse whinnied and nodded when she petted his neck and spoke softly to him.

The other two were mares, one a roan named Red Lady, the other a gray speckled horse named Queen. Clint claimed both were easy to handle, especially Queen.

"I have a question, Clint," she spoke up, coming closer to watch him again.

He put an arm over Devil's neck and faced her. "What's that?"

"You've never told me how old you are."

He grinned, and she thought how nice it was to be around him when he was in a good mood. However, she couldn't help wondering if it was only because he was finally on his way to find another wanted man.

"How old do you *think* I am?"

She shrugged, pulling her cape closer. The day was cool and damp. "I can't decide. Early thirties, maybe?"

"Thirty on the head," he answered. "I guess you to be about eighteen."

"I'm twenty," she answered. She saw more questions in his eyes. He probably wondered why she was still single. A man like Clint couldn't possibly understand that the work of the Lord must come before personal wants and needs.

He turned away. "You mean you didn't leave behind some broken hearts when you left San Francisco?"

"Oh, there were a couple of interested young men, but I didn't share the interest." She took a deep breath and looked out at the mountains. "The man I marry will have to be very special, a Christian man who shares my faith and puts God above all else, a steady, settled man who knows his Bible and who will be a good provider and a wonderful father. He'll have to be brave like my father was, brave enough to voice his faith among the unfaithful. And of course he'll be strong and handsome and—"

She suddenly realized how she'd been rambling, like a silly girl fantasizing about a prince. She glanced at Clint and realized that he fit at least part of her description— strong and handsome and brave—but brave in the ways of violence. She felt heat come into her cheeks, and she covered her face. "I'm sorry! That was silly of me."

The words were met by silence. What was he thinking? Did he wonder if she was describing him? Or was he insulted, thinking he didn't fit any of that description? And why on earth did she care *what* he thought!

"Nothing wrong with being particular," he finally answered.

She uncovered her face, and he'd returned to his packing.

"One thing I forgot to tell you," he said, obviously trying to change the subject. "No dresses. We need to go find you some pants that will fit you. Small as you are, that won't be easy. We might have to shop for boy's pants."

"Pants! I can't wear pants! It isn't proper!"

He stopped his packing and faced her, again wearing his "don't argue with me" look. "Where we're headed, lady, you'll be walking knee-deep, maybe sometimes *waist*-deep in snow. I don't think I need to paint any better picture than that. I'll not have you end up with frostbite clear up to—" He looked her over, and Elizabeth felt like a complete idiot for not realizing why she'd have to wear pants. "You get my meaning," he finished. He dug into his pocket and handed her some money. "Here. Go shopping."

"Clint, you've already done too much. I'll never in the world be able to pay you back."

"And I've told you not to worry about it." He took hold of one of her hands and shoved the money into it. "Once I find the man I'm looking for, money will be the least of my worries for quite a while. And like I said before, what the heck else would I be spending it on?" He turned away again to strap on the last bit of supplies. "I have no home," he continued, "no property but my horses and gear, and no one to leave my money to anyway. I might as well spend it any way I want, and right now I feel like spending it on helping you get to Dawson. Now go buy yourself some pants and a warm coat and wool hat, and boots, and anything else that will ensure your warmth. Then go back to the hotel room. I'll put away the horses and store this gear for the night and meet you in the hotel lobby in the morning. We can pack your remaining personal supplies then. And make sure you bring along enough…you know…woman things."

She frowned. "Woman things? You said yourself I can't wear dresses."

He rolled his eyes again. "I'm not talking about dresses. I was married once, you know. I know about those things. Make sure you bring enough supplies along for that time of the month."

Elizabeth was so embarrassed she wanted to die! She couldn't look at him as he mounted one of his horses. "See you in the morning," he told her. He took the reins to the other two horses and rode off.

Elizabeth just stood there, dumbfounded that the man had even thought about "woman things." Embarrassing as it was, it drove home the fact that she'd be traveling with a man far more experienced and worldly than she'd ever known.

"Oh, Lord," she said with a sigh, "how can someone like me get through to a man like that?"

Just as quickly as the thought had come, so did a little voice inside that reminded her of the horrendous task God had given His own Son, Jesus Christ…to die a horrible death on the cross to save sinners like Clint Brady. There could be no greater burden. Jesus had sweat blood in agony over that burden the night before his death. Finding a way to get through to Clint Brady's heart was not so much to ask.

Chapter Twenty-One

*There is one lawgiver, who is able to save and to
destroy; who art thou that judgest another?*
—James 4:12

Elizabeth watched her footing as she led Queen along the
foothills of White Pass Trail north of Skagway. The ground
was a combination of grass and rock, ranging anywhere
from pebbles to much larger boulders. Such cascades of
rock meant they were constantly in danger of being crushed
to death if they were not on a minute-by-minute lookout
for the next tumbling killer.

All of this made it impossible to hurry along the trail. A
steady walk was all they could muster. They were forced to
travel even slower in places where the trail narrowed to
hardly more than a pathway around the side of a precarious
ledge. Elizabeth tried not to look down for fear of fainting.

Keeping watch both above for tumbling rocks and on the
ground under their feet for smaller rocks that could cause

them to lose their footing, kept both Clint and Elizabeth on edge. Elizabeth's feet ached from the long day's walk, and her neck and back ached, mostly, she figured, from fatigue and tension. Clint was worried about how easily his horses could suffer wounds to their hooves or legs.

Elizabeth in turn worried about Clint, who she felt was still not rested and well enough to make this trip. However, there was no arguing with him about it. She could not imagine that finding one man could be worth the misery they were sure to be heading into, and she hoped that secretly he was doing this more for her sake than to find a wanted man. But from what she'd seen so far, money meant more to most men than anything else. Why else would they leave wives and children and comfortable homes and good jobs to literally risk their lives reaching their El Dorado, especially when it was likely most of them would never strike it rich?

Gold. The Bible itself was filled with kings and slaves, untold wealth and horrible poverty. In one parable Jesus had said it would be easier for a camel to go through the eye of a needle than for a rich man to get to heaven, although her father had always taught that what the Lord meant was rich men who refused to share their wealth and who committed sins to obtain and hang on to their wealth. There were generous, compassionate rich men, just far fewer of them than those who would give up just about anything for wealth.

The sad part about Clint was that she suspected the money didn't really matter to him as much as simply finding a wanted man and doing away with him. That was what bothered her most, the obvious deep hurt and hatred in the man that led him to continue the hunt, man after man, as though each new find might somehow be the answer to finding his own peace.

"May I ask just who it is you are looking for?" she spoke up, hoping to relieve the constant tension over the dangers they faced, as well as the unnerving silence. They had walked the last two miles or so without speaking at all.

Clint led the way, although the already well-worn trail, in this second year of the gold rush, was easy to follow on this sunny day. Other pack trains were about a mile ahead of them, which meant that besides watching for rocks, one had to be on the lookout for horse manure.

"His name is Roland Fisher," Clint yelled back. "He's an Eskimo, a half-breed, actually, from up in the Yukon."

"What in the world was he doing down in the States?"

Clint didn't answer right away. They made it to a wide, flat area, where he stopped and looked back at her. "Let's rest the horses for a while." He glanced at the sun, which was getting very close to settling behind a distant peak. "Actually this would be a good place to make camp." He looked around at dark circles on the ground where others had made fires. "Apparently a lot of others thought the same thing. And I think there is a party a ways behind us. They just might end up reaching this place, too. We'd better go ahead and pick the best spot." He walked Devil closer to a sheer wall of rock. "We'll camp here so we'll be out of the way of any others who might decide to head on past us."

This was their very first night on the trail, and one thing Elizabeth was more sure of was that she didn't have to worry about Clint Brady getting any funny ideas in regards to tenting alone together. She had no doubt he was just as tired as she, and that his feet were just as sore as hers were, and that he shared her craving for a good night's sleep.

Clint began untying the ropes that held the canvas tent he'd brought along and continued his explanation of the man he hunted. "Rather than take the chance of never striking it rich in the Klondike when the gold rush began, Fisher decided to go to Skagway and see if he couldn't find a 'get rich quick' job there by taking advantage of all the gold seekers, like any smart man would do."

"What does that have to do with ending up in the States?" she asked.

"Grab the other end of this thing and help me open it up," Clint answered, unfolding the tent. He was breathing heavily and he stopped to cough before he continued. "He was hired to help guard a shipment of gold nuggets on its way to San Francisco. The job paid well, so he took it. The shipment left too late in the year for him to think about coming back before winter, so he stayed on in California, taking a job helping guard a stamping mill at one of the mines northeast of San Francisco."

With the tent all laid out, Clint took down a burlap sack that contained iron tent stakes, then yanked a sledge hammer from its stirrup. He began pounding the stakes into the hard earth, not an easy job, and one Elizabeth knew for certain she never could have done herself.

"Come this past spring," he continued, "Fisher for some reason decided to rob the very bank where he'd been cashing his pay checks. It was situated in a little town north of San Francisco." After finishing one stake, he went on to the next. "He was easy to identify because he'd been there several times. The teller he shot told the authorities who'd shot him…" He looked over at Elizabeth. "Before he died." He returned to hammering. "That teller was a fairly young man with three little kids. He left behind a kind wife and mother who will have a heck of a time raising those kids alone." He stood up and went on to the next stake. "The bank owner, the owner of the stamp mill and some of the teller's friends pooled their money to come up with the reward for Fisher…dead or alive."

Elizabeth relieved Queen of some of her load. "But why would he work guarding gold all that time, apparently being well paid for it, and then just suddenly decide to rob a bank? It doesn't make sense."

Clint rose to walk over to a fourth stake. "A lot of things in life don't make sense. Maybe he just missed home and decided to go back a little richer than he already was. According to what he'd told others he worked with, he had a wife and a couple of kids up in the Yukon. Maybe he figured if he went back there, nobody would follow him that far."

Elizabeth set out a coffeepot. "But you will."

He pounded on the fourth stake. "Why not? I don't have anything better to do, and I feel sorry for the widow who was left behind. I know what it's like to lose one's mate to violence."

A clue. His wife had died violently. The son, too? Elizabeth unpacked bedrolls. "I'm sorry you understand that kind of sorrow. Still, don't you worry about possibly killing an innocent man? I mean, it just doesn't make sense, a man leaving a wife and children to work hard to support them, and then just up and robbing a bank."

"You already said that. And no, I'm not worried about his innocence, because I know he's guilty. The teller identified him, and that's good enough for me. I'll find him and I'll take him back, dead or alive, just like the poster says. That's what I do for a living." Clint rose and walked over to pound in a fifth stake.

"So, because of a poster, you have the right to be judge and jury and hangman?"

He pounded extra hard on the fifth stake. "I told you— no preaching."

Elizabeth walked closer and shoved a support post under the front section of the tent, pushing up on it to raise the front opening. "I'm not preaching this time. Just sort of thinking out loud, I guess."

Clint continued to the sixth stake. "You're the one who says we shouldn't judge, so don't judge *me*, Liz."

"I'm not doing that, either. I'm just trying to figure out why you do what you do." She walked around behind the tent to secure a pole there, hoping she could keep him talking so she could learn more about the complexities of the man. After all…unwanted feelings for him were growing deep inside. How could she possibly allow such feelings for a bounty hunter, of all men? "You just don't seem like the typical kind of man who would choose to be a bounty hunter."

"You've already made that clear, more than once. And quit trying to get information out of me." He pounded in the seventh stake.

Elizabeth began stretching rope from the top of one of the poles to a stake to hold it up. "Foiled again," she answered, hoping to keep the conversation light. One thing she did know was that Clint Brady could become sullen and angry over one wrong word, and they had a long trip ahead of them. She caught a grin at the corner of his mouth and felt relieved that she'd managed to keep to his lighter side.

"I'll finish the tent," he told her. "You take more of the load off Queen and Red Lady and tether them. I'll try to get a fire going. Some hot coffee sounds good right now. So does a good night's sleep."

"Agreed," she answered. She studied the tent a moment. It was meant for two people, but certainly not much else. It was going to feel very awkward sleeping in a cramped tent with a man who was not her husband or even related to her. Then again, she might as well *be* a man, the way she was dressed: woolen pants that were slightly too big for her, a red flannel shirt that was also too big, then covered with a canvas coat, a woolen hat, high leather boots over thick woolen socks, her hair twisted into a bun at the base of her neck so she could pull her hat completely over it… *Lord, I must be just about the most unattractive woman in all of Alaska right now,* she thought.

She walked back to Queen, taking a moment to look out at the stretch of mountains and valleys all around. It would all be so beautiful if it were not so dangerous. Yet she couldn't help feeling safe. She was with Clint Brady.

Bounty hunter or not, he was a strong, able man, and God had led them together. She trusted God above all else…and so she would trust Clint.

Chapter Twenty-Two

These...things doth the Lord hate:... A false witness that speaketh lies, and he that soweth discord among brethren.
—Proverbs 6:16 & 19

"Hello there!"

Elizabeth looked up to see another party of gold seekers approaching. She and Clint sat beside a campfire in front of their tent, and, in spite of the interruption to their quietude, Elizabeth was actually relieved by the visit. For the past hour or so, she'd been fighting the embarrassment of going inside the tent and settling down to sleep beside Clint. She had a feeling he felt just as awkward about it, so they had both lingered by the fire after eating boiled pork and potatoes. The sun was long set, but neither of them had made a move to retire, in spite of being bone-tired.

"I see you have horses," one of the men spoke up. He

walked into the light of the fire, and Clint, wearing his sidearm, rose defensively.

"That's right," he answered.

"Well, if it isn't the son of a bitch who punched me out a couple of nights ago!" the visitor spoke up then.

Alarmed, Elizabeth also rose, realizing there could be trouble. She moved to stand beside Clint. The visitor, Ezra Faine, looked her over, then moved his gaze back to Clint. Behind Ezra stood at least six other men.

"I see the woman found someone to travel with," he nearly sneered at Clint.

"The woman is my wife," Clint answered.

Faine's eyebrows arched in surprise. "*Wife!* You two got married?"

"That's right." Clint put his hands on his hips. "Now, you've commented about my horses and Mrs. Brady, neither of which is your business, so you can keep on going."

Faine stiffened. He glanced back at the others, a couple of whom chuckled. It was obvious Ezra Faine was the leader of the pack of men, all of them carting heavy loads on their backs and traveling completely on foot.

Faine eyed Clint again. "It's dark. Surely you don't expect us to keep going. Any one of us could lose our footing and fall a thousand feet."

"Am I supposed to care?"

"Clint!" Elizabeth spoke up. "There is plenty of room in this clearing. Surely there is nothing wrong with letting them make camp here."

Clint cast her a look of anger and chastisement. "After what this man said to you a couple of days ago?"

"Well, it…it just wouldn't be Christian to make them keep going in the dark."

Faine smiled and tipped his hat to her. "How kind of you, ma'am. And I do apologize for my remarks the other night. I deserved a wallop from your husband."

Elizabeth raised her chin. "You most certainly did."

Faine, his left cheek still visibly bruised and swollen, grinned and faced Clint again. "Friends?"

"No," Clint answered. "But you can make camp here if you want. It's public land. Just stay well away from this tent…and my horses."

Faine chuckled as though it was a great joke. He turned to his cohorts and told them to go ahead and make camp. Their eyes adjusted to the near darkness, and with a three-quarter moon above, the men were able to find an area out of the light of Clint and Elizabeth's campfire.

"Now, about the horses," Faine spoke up to Clint.

"What about them?"

"Well, as you must know, procuring a horse in Skagway is near impossible. Every available horse is grabbed up as fast as it comes off a boat, and for unheard-of prices. In light of that, and the length of this journey, and the weight of our packs, I thought you might be willing to sell at least one horse to us. I am willing to pay four hundred dollars, far more than any of your horses is worth, I might add."

"Maybe in the States," Clint answered. "But on a trail from Skagway to Dawson, you couldn't get me to sell for a *thousand* dollars. Besides that, I've owned these horses for years. They were mine before I even left San Francisco, and they aren't for sale at any price."

Looking angry and chagrined, Faine pursed his lips mockingly. He sighed deeply, looking Clint over. "Well, you can't blame a man for trying."

"There are a lot of things a man can be blamed for," Clint retorted. "Why don't you just go join your friends. And, by the way, I'm a light sleeper."

Faine frowned. "Mr. Brady! Are you saying you don't trust me?"

"That's exactly what I'm saying."

"Clint, the man apologized," Elizabeth spoke up.

"He didn't mean a word of it." Clint nodded toward the others. "Go join the rest of your party," he told Faine.

Faine sighed deeply, glancing at Elizabeth again. "Thank you for at least trying to be hospitable, ma'am. And again, I apologize." He backed away. "And I must say, I can't imagine such a nice young lady marrying such a rude, unfriendly man as Mr. Brady." He took another look at both of them, eyeing Clint's gun for a moment, then left.

Elizabeth turned to Clint. "If they had any bad intentions, you certainly didn't help any with your attitude," she chastised.

Clint grasped her arm a little too tightly and made her sit down on the log they'd been sharing. "Look, I can be as friendly as the next man with people who deserve it. That man doesn't. The rest of them might be all right, but not that one. And it's my bet they all would follow just about anything he told them to do. When it comes to handling men like that, let *me* take care of it. Understood?"

"But a kind word—"

"Understood?"

"Let go of my arm."

Clint sighed deeply, doing as she asked. His tone softened, and he leaned closer. "You have to admit that I know a bit more about these things than you, right?"

Elizabeth frowned. "That doesn't mean you have to be rude to people."

"It does when my gut instinct tells me someone isn't worth trusting," he said, keeping his voice down. "And after dealing with some of the worst of them, my instinct is honed pretty darn well. And I'm telling you that Mr. Manners over there would steal my horses, and you along with them, if he got the chance. Fact is, we're staying an extra day and letting that bunch of fast talkers go on ahead of us. I don't intend to travel with them at my back. Got that? And from now on, when strangers come along, I'll be the judge of who we're friendly with and who we aren't. When men come along to test out your vulnerability, especially when you have something they want, you let them know right up front that you're not to be messed with."

Elizabeth blinked back tears of anger and embarrassment. "It's hard for me to be unfriendly," she answered, her voice quivering. To her surprise, he moved an arm around her shoulders, giving her a reassuring hug.

"Well, it isn't hard for me, so let me do the talking, all right? I'm not asking you to do or say anything you don't feel right about. I'm just asking you to be still and let me handle things. Will you *please* do that?"

Elizabeth nodded. She quickly wiped at a tear. "Do you really think they might cause trouble?"

He gave her one more squeeze before pulling a pre-rolled cigarette from his jacket pocket. "I don't know. I only know I don't trust them, and that these horses are as valuable to us as the air we breathe." He lit the cigarette with a burning stick from the fire. "Sometimes when you set a man straight right off, it saves a lot of trouble later." He took a long, quiet drag on the cigarette. "Now why don't you go inside the tent and try to sleep. I intend to keep an eye on things for a while. And bury yourself good into the sleeping bag. It gets mighty cold in these higher elevations at night, and I intend to open one side of the back of the tent and tether the horses back there...to my ankle. Anybody tries anything, I'll know it right quick."

"It isn't good for you to breathe such cold air."

"I'll wrap a woolen scarf around my face. I'll be fine. I've slept out in colder weather. You're the one who isn't used to it."

Elizabeth finished a cup of coffee and rose. "I'm sorry I interfered."

"Don't worry about it. Just get some sleep. I might need you to wake up early morning and keep watch while *I* get some sleep. We're not leaving until that bunch gets a good head start on us."

Elizabeth felt almost sick from being sore and tired. "If that's what you want." She headed for the tent, going inside and grimacing as she removed her boots. She rubbed her sore feet for a few minutes, then crawled into her blankets, pulling them up over her head as Clint had ordered. She thought how at least the incident had dispelled her nervousness about sharing a tent this first night with Clint. It would likely be a while before he even came inside to sleep. By the time he did, she'd be asleep herself. After tonight, things wouldn't seem so awkward. She just had to get used to it.

"God, watch over him," she prayed. *"Please don't let there be any trouble."*

Chapter Twenty-Three

Deliver me, oh Lord, from the evil man:
preserve me from the violent man...
—Psalms 140:1

Elizabeth awoke to birds singing. She sat up, noticing Clint was not inside the tent. The last she remembered, he was sitting inside smoking, and told her he would take his bedroll outside and sleep there so he could keep an eye on the horses.

She shivered from the cold, thinking how much colder it must have been lying outside in the damp air. She took the combs from her hair and shook it out, then rewound it into a bun and fastened it. Looking down at her pants, she wondered how she must look to others. By the time this trip was over, she'd be an even worse mess from not being able to bathe or wash her hair. She wondered already if she could ever feel or look feminine again.

She pulled on her boots and jacket and crawled out of the tent. Clint sat by a renewed fire, drinking coffee and smoking yet another cigarette. She stood up, rubbing her eyes.

"Finally woke up, did you?" Clint teased.

Elizabeth stretched. "Did you ever sleep?"

"Some."

"You're going to make yourself sick again, Clint."

"I bundled up plenty good. As you can see, our horses are still here."

She glanced at Devil, Queen and Red Lady, then over toward Ezra Faine's camp. The men there were packing up. "I see," she answered. "I really don't think it was necessary for you to lie out in the damp cold all night."

"Well, I *do* think it was. And we'll wait right here until those fellows over there get a good head start on us. You might as well fix us some breakfast. I might even try getting a couple more hours' sleep while you take a turn watching the horses. It will put us somewhat behind, but I'd rather that bunch went on ahead. It will be worth it."

Elizabeth shook her head. "Whatever you say." She headed over to a cluster of rocks behind which she had no choice but to drop her trousers and drawers to relieve herself. If nothing else, this trip would certainly damage her modesty, that was sure. And it would be a while before she felt halfway comfortable in such a position with an unrelated man nearby. She walked back to the campfire and dug a frying pan out of their gear. "Pork and potatoes?"

"Sounds good." Clint was watching the Faine party.

Elizabeth set up a sheet-iron stove and set a black fry

pan over the flames. She dropped in a few pieces of pork, which created enough grease to fry potatoes. She quickly sliced some into the pan, then sat down next to Clint. He poured coffee into a tin cup and handed it to her.

"Thanks for making this," she told him. "Sorry I didn't get up sooner."

He shrugged, keeping the cigarette between his lips. "Didn't matter this morning, since we aren't leaving right away. The horses can probably use the rest, too." He removed the cigarette and drank some coffee, and Elizabeth noticed he wore his six-gun and kept a rifle beside him. "I'll take a bucket to a little waterfall I found in some rocks just around the bend of the trail," he added. "I'll fill it for the horses. I found the waterfall earlier when I walked a little ways ahead." He took one more drag and threw the butt of the cigarette into the fire, then looked at her with a mixture of humor and warning in his eyes. "You won't believe what's just around the bend."

Why did his closeness stir such odd feelings deep inside…a desire to touch him? Elizabeth had to turn her attention to the cooking food. It was difficult to look into those startlingly blue eyes; the man was so handsome in spite of the fact that he already needed a shave. He'd probably have a pretty good beard by the time they reached Dawson.

She stirred the food. "What's around the bend?"

"A view like nothing either of us has ever seen, even though we've seen the Sierras," he answered. "It would be beautiful if not for the fact that we have to go through it. We have three pretty challenging mountains to get across before we reach Lake Bennett, which is where we'll finally be able to finish the trip by way of the Yukon River. But that's a good fifty miles off, and the last climb will be White Pass. From around the bend you can see it, and *white* is a good description. There's a lot of snow up there, Elizabeth. We could lose all three of the horses before we even get there, narrow as the trail is in some places—and it's almost for sure we'll lose them trying to get over the pass."

Elizabeth looked back at Clint's loyal steeds. It was only natural to be attached already, and she realized Clint must be much more attached than she. She knelt by the fire and kept stirring. "I'm sorry. Clint, if you want to go back—"

"No. We'll make it, horses or no horses. But since you have some kind of an in with God, it wouldn't hurt for you to keep praying those three mounts make it, at least to the top of White Pass."

She smiled and looked over at him. "I don't have an *in,* as you put it. But I will do my best." She stirred the potatoes again. "I'd hate for you to lose your horses."

He sighed deeply, watching the Faine party finish their packing. "I can buy more."

So, you won't even let yourself get attached to your faithful animals for fear of losing them, Elizabeth thought. Or at least you pretend not to care.

Clint remained silent as she finished cooking the pork and potatoes. She scooped some onto a tin plate for him and handed it to him with a fork. By then Ezra Faine and those with him were ready to head out, their backs packed heavily. Two men were hitched to a sled like draft animals. They left, passing Clint and Elizabeth on the way. Ezra stopped to address them.

"Shouldn't you two be underway?" he asked with a frown. "There's no time to waste this time of year."

"We'll be along," Clint answered. "I figured I'd let you go first. Wouldn't want to hold you up."

Faine pretended an unconcerned laugh. "You just want us ahead of you, is that it?"

Clint handed his plate to Elizabeth, taking hold of his rifle and placing it over his knees. "Something like that."

"Not exactly the friendly sort, are you?" one of the other men commented.

"Depends on who wants to be friendly," Clint answered. "Word is there are men on these trips who would kill for horses and supplies. I'm just looking out for my own."

"Probably a good idea," another spoke up. It was Jonathan Hedley.

Clint just nodded. "Good luck," he told them.

Faine glanced at Elizabeth, then back to Clint. "Same to you." Again he looked at Elizabeth. "If anything should happen to your...uh...*husband* there...we won't be far ahead, ma'am, if you should need help."

"Thank you," Elizabeth answered. She realized the man didn't believe their story about getting married. If not, did they still think her a wanton woman? "I'm sure we'll be fine."

Faine tipped his hat. "Let's go, men." He plodded on, and the others followed. Elizabeth noticed that Clint watched them until the last man was out of sight around the bend. Then he rose.

"I'm going to make sure they do keep going," he told Elizabeth.

"Clint, just finish your food. It will get cold."

"Put it back in the pan till I get back. It'll keep," he answered.

He picked up his rifle and headed for an outcropping of rocks that hid the trail beyond. Elizabeth looked out at the surrounding mountains, now lighting up from the morning sun. Along the lower elevations across the wide chasm from where they were camped burst a display of splendid color from golden aspens that still hung on to their leaves, mixed with dark-green spruce and crimson undergrowth splashed with the purple and white of flowering autumn weeds. It was all so beautiful against the snowy mountains that rose above the color. She saw something move, then squinted her eyes to focus more sharply on the image.

"A bear," she said softly. It looked small from where she stood, but she surmised it would be much bigger up close. She hoped she'd never find out if that was so.

"What's so interesting?" Clint shouted.

She turned to see him returning. "There's a bear down there," she said, pointing.

Clint walked closer, and it took him a few seconds to see where she was pointing. "Yup, I see it. Looks like a grizzly." He grunted a laugh. "Better there than here."

Elizabeth smiled in agreement. "Look at the colors, Clint. It's so beautiful!"

He looked out at the scene with her, and she thought how in that little moment they shared something. She could feel a little part of what must have been the "old" Clint Brady, a man who could relax and appreciate beauty, but the moment did not last long.

"It's deceiving," he said, suddenly turning away. "Beneath all that beauty is a lot of danger. Come on. I'll finish eating. You can enjoy the view while I get some extra sleep."

Chapter Twenty-Four

*Blessed be the Lord my strength... My goodness
and my fortress; my high tower, and my deliverer;
my shield, and He in whom I trust...*
—Psalms 144:1 & 2

For the next two days the journey became so treacherous that there was little time for talk. Sleeping in the same tent with Clint no longer worried Elizabeth. Both fell exhausted into their blankets at night, and the exertion had made Clint's cough worse again, so that he was even more drained at night than Elizabeth.

She was glad she'd brought along the smelly liniment. She'd heated it for him, and he'd smeared the mysterious, oily concoction onto his chest himself. He hadn't even wanted to smoke, which was a relief to Elizabeth, who was not so sure smoking wasn't sinful, let alone surely not good for a man. But knowing Clint, he would not care to hear her preach against the habit. *If only that was his only fault.*

On the third day, they reached the first corduroy bridge across the foaming, freezing and very intimidating Skagway River.

"The guide I talked to said we'd have to cross several of these bridges to get to White Pass," Clint yelled to Elizabeth above the roar of the churning water. "After that we'll be in British Columbia."

The memory of her near-drowning came vividly to Elizabeth's mind. She never wanted to experience such a thing again, and the force of the river surely meant it would be impossible to survive the current if one fell in. Apparently Clint saw the fear in her eyes as she stared at the roaring death trap. He walked back to where she stood.

"I'll take the horses across first, then come back for you," he told her. "Don't worry. Thousands of other men and horses have crossed these things."

"Clint, be careful!" she told him. "If you fall into those waters and don't drown, you'll be sick all over again!"

He buttoned his fur-lined coat higher to his neck. The water's spray in this area made it seem colder than it really was. "Don't worry," he told her. He took hold of Devil's harness and started across the wobbly log bridge, constantly talking to the black gelding to keep him calm. Elizabeth's heart nearly stopped beating when the horse whinnied and balked, rearing back slightly and nearly pushing Clint off the bridge.

Clint managed to calm the animal and get him to the other side, a process that took a good ten minutes. He tied Devil to a little pine tree that jutted out of the rocks nearby and balanced his way back across the bridge to repeat the process with Queen and Red Lady. The sweeter-tempered mares caused much less trouble than Devil. Clint tied them and returned for Elizabeth.

"It's not that bad," he told her. "If those horses could make it across, you sure can."

"I should have just come across behind you the second time," she told him. "It's just the memory of falling off the *Damsel*."

"Don't worry about it." Clint moved his right arm around her back, grasping her waist for extra support, then grasped the rope railing with his left hand. Elizabeth clung to the right-side rope and they made their way carefully across the precarious logs. She could not help appreciating the strength of Clint's grasp, and she thought how it seemed like God protecting her through this man.

"Yea, though I walk through the valley of the shadow of death," she shouted.

Clint laughed lightly. He gave her a light squeeze, which surprised her...and was sinfully pleasing. It amazed her that she could think of that in such a time of fear and peril, but it was Clint helping her, reassuring her, risking his life, money and belongings for her. How could she not begin to feel an attachment? Was the same thing happening to him?

She reminded herself he was doing this mainly to reach Dawson so he could hunt for a wanted man. Still, already she was wondering what things would be like once they reached Dawson. Would he simply hunt down Roland Fisher and either kill him or tie him to his horse and leave? Would their own relationship, such as it was, simply end with a thank-you and a goodbye?

The security of his arm around her was unlike anything she'd felt before. It wasn't like a hug from her mother or father, or her brother. It was much more…dangerously more…dangerous because of the things that were happening to her heart, things that absolutely should *not* be happening, let alone so soon into their friendship, if it could even be called that.

They reached the other side safely, to Elizabeth's great relief. It also struck her that she'd been so lost in thought that she hardly remembered most of the frightening short jaunt over the bridge.

"On to the next bridge," he told her, letting go of her. He walked up and untied the horses, bringing them to the edge of the tumbling waters so they could take a drink. As he waited, he looked her over, smiling. "Have I ever told you how utterly ridiculous you look in those clothes?"

She looked down at herself and laughed. "I'm sure I do."

"And now do you understand why I said you had to wear pants and boots? Can you imagine trying to get across that bridge wearing a bunch of slips and petticoats, let alone making your way over this rocky trail?"

"Oh, I do understand," she answered, taking Queen's reins. Clint tied Red Lady to Devil's tail, then grasped Devil's reins and started off again. Elizabeth followed him along a trail that meandered along the opposite side of the river. She always felt easier around Clint when he was in this kind of mood, and she felt better now about the log bridges. The next one would be easier, she knew, because Clint would never let her fall.

For the rest of that third day the trail led them along

endlessly steep gorges, again and again meeting the Skagway River, over more log bridges, the pathway widening, then narrowing again to widths that made Elizabeth's chest tighten. It was difficult to believe they were hardly halfway to the height they must reach at White Pass. They still were not even above the tree line, and she tried not to think about what lay ahead in the awesome, dark granite, angular peaks. When she looked up at the vast bastions of the frigid interior of Alaska and Canada, starkly outlined against a deep-blue sky, she wondered that any man could surmount them, but thousands had, and so would she and Clint.

They moved past rocks that literally seemed to leak trickles of water, as well as splendid waterfalls that roared in Elizabeth's ears. They stopped only briefly at midday for something to eat, then headed into an area where the trail widened considerably, much to Elizabeth's relief. Trees and underbrush gave way to a clearing, where they spotted several men with instruments set up on tripods.

"Surveyors," Clint shouted back to Elizabeth.

They approached the men, one wearing spectacles, all well-dressed and equipped for camping in the area. They hailed Clint and Elizabeth with friendly gestures.

"How has the trip been so far?" the man with glasses asked Clint.

"As good as can be expected," Clint answered. He reached back for Elizabeth. "My name is Clint Brady, and this is my wife, Elizabeth."

The man nodded to her and then turned his gaze to Clint again. "Robert Stokes. We're with the Northern Pacific and are trying to build a railroad to the Yukon so you people don't have to make this trip on foot and horseback."

"A railroad! Into country like this?" Elizabeth asked.

Stokes laughed. "That's what they said back in the sixties when men proposed a transcontinental railroad through the Rockies and the Sierras. But wherever men go, especially when it involves gold, the railroad will follow, ma'am, no matter the obstacles. Never underestimate us."

"Oh, I wouldn't think of it," Elizabeth replied.

"Have many others passed by you today?" Clint asked.

"Two parties—both inexperienced men who have no business trying this trip, but you know gold and men. I suppose that's your purpose also."

"Actually no," Clint answered. "My wife is looking for her brother, who went to Dawson over a year ago to preach, believe it or not. Me, I'm...well, I agreed to take her, simple as that."

Stokes looked him over, studied the pack horses. "Well, you sure don't look like a man inexperienced at this kind of trip."

"I did my share of living under the stars before I got married," Clint answered, with no further explanation. "By the way, was one of the parties who passed by here led by a man named Ezra Faine?"

Stokes nodded. "About four hours ahead of you. He tried to buy a couple of horses from us, but they belong to the railroad. I've got no right to sell them."

Clint nodded, then tipped his floppy-brimmed, leather hat to them. "Thanks. Good luck to you."

"Same to you. There's an even better clearing about an